The Slum Angel Christmas

AnneMarie Brear

AnneMarie Brear

Contents

Historical

To Gain What's Lost
Isabelle's Choice
Nicola's Virtue
Aurora's Pride
Grace's Courage
Eden's Conflict
Catrina's Return
Broken Hero
The Promise of Tomorrow
The Slum Angel
Beneath a Stormy Sky
The Tobacconist's Wife

Kitty McKenzie Series

Kitty McKenzie
Kitty McKenzie's Land
Southern Sons

Marsh Saga Series

Millie
Christmas at the Chateau
Prue
Cece

The Beaumont Series

The Market Stall Girl
The Woman from Beaumont Farm

The Distant Series

A Distant Horizon
Beyond the Distant Hills

Contemporary

Long Distance Love
Hooked on You

Chapter One

Bedern Slums, York, England. November 1881

In the muted grey light of dawn which crept over the dim room from the only window, Georgiana Carter wiped the blood away from the tiny face of her newborn son. The church bells around the ancient city rang out five times, waking its inhabitants from their slumber to begin another day.

Puffing from the strain of giving birth, Georgiana leaned back against the cold wall and inwardly gave thanks for the safe delivery of her baby and that it was also morning, and she could knock on the wall for her neighbour, Doris Turner, or Dorrie as everyone in the tenements called her. As the weak light lifted the darkness, the room came into focus, reminding her of the poverty she lived amongst.

Shivering, she pulled the threadbare blanket up over her bare legs, trying to find some warmth in a freezing cold room. The small fire was nothing but dull winking embers in the grate. She really should shift herself and put more pieces of coke onto the fire before it went out completely as she didn't have any matches or bits of wood to start another.

A cup of tea would be wonderful, but the water buckets were empty, like the shelves on the wall. She had no money for food or rent this week. Would her husband, Roly, be home soon, his pockets bursting with coins from his wages? His boat was due in last week but still hadn't arrived at the King's Staith dock on the River Ouse. She needed him home desperately.

Grabbing a tin cup from the rickety table by the iron bed, Georgiana banged on the wall several times knowing Dorrie would be up now and ushering her large family to get out of bed and eat whatever food she put in front of them before they took themselves off to work or school.

While waiting, Georgiana wrapped her son into a worn thin blanket and laid him in the crook of one arm while she pushed again and expelled the afterbirth. She glanced quickly at her six-year-old daughter, Iris, who slept beside her, and who hadn't woken despite her mother's groans during the night while the labour progressed.

This had been Georgiana's third pregnancy and the labour had been bearable and thankfully short. Her first pains started late yesterday evening and she'd walked the floor for a few hours before getting into bed before dawn. Twenty minutes of pushing, biting on a wooden spoon so she wouldn't wake Iris or her neighbours, and finally her little son was born. From experience she knew to have twine and a sharp knife close by to tie and cut the cord.

She named the baby Francis, after her late grandfather, but would call him Frankie. He fed at her breast for five minutes before falling asleep.

The door opened, for it was never locked, and Dorrie walked in, beaming as she saw the baby and the evidence of birth.

'All right, lass?' Dorrie whispered.

'Aye. All good.'

'You should have woken me.'

'I didn't want to disturb you or the others.'

The older woman tutted. 'They'd have gone back to sleep quick enough.'

'Can you check the afterbirth? I think it's come out in one piece.'

'Let us have a gander at it then.' Dorrie, having had twelve pregnancies, knew everything there was to carrying and delivering babies. She stretched out the afterbirth. 'It looks fine to me. No holes or bits missing. Get up and walk about, lass. Get the blood flowing out. It's better out than in.' Dorrie took a cloth and dipped it in the bowl beside the bed and wiped the blood from Georgiana's thighs before helping her into a pair of flannel drawers and tying a sanitary pad to a belt around her waist.

Carefully, her legs a little wobbly and feeling a bit off balance at first, Georgiana soon paced the square room, feeling the birth blood come away, *cleansing* as Dorrie put it.

Footsteps sounded outside Georgiana's door, echoing into her small room that was her home on the second floor of the Birch House tenement. Their room was just one of the dozens housing hundreds of people who lived in poverty and destitution in the middle of York.

Dorrie went to the door and opened it to lean out and shout. 'Danny, get me some water.' She then folded up the soiled newspaper laid to protect the mattress and stuck it in the fire.

Moments later, Danny, Dorrie's third oldest son, stuck his bleary-eyed head around the door. 'What do you want, Ma?'

'Here.' She thrust two empty buckets at him. 'Water and tell Harry I want a bucket of coke brought in.'

'I'll be late for work, Ma,' he complained.

'You'll be going to work with a slap up the side of your head if you don't get a move on.' Dorrie gave him one of her stern looks which her children young and old knew meant business.

Dorrie's four oldest children were married and living in various parts of York, but she still had eight children living at home with her and her invalided husband Sam. She ruled not just her family with a rod of iron but the entire tenement building. Big-hearted, she was loved and admired, but also respected. Dorrie was known to give a lending hand to others without question and share whatever she had available, which usually wasn't much with her large family.

Still, Georgiana didn't know where she'd be without her wonderful neighbour.

She returned to the bed as Iris woke and sat quietly rubbing the sleep from her eyes. 'Look, darling, you have a baby brother.'

Iris smiled and touched a little finger to her brother's soft cheek. 'Baby brother.'

'We'll call him, Frankie,' Georgiana told her, climbing back into bed to get warm.

Dorrie thanked Harry who brought in a bucket of coke on his way to work. 'Have a good day, lad.' Dorrie gave him a loving smile before stirring up the fire to get a warm blaze going, enough at least to warm the kettle. 'When Danny brings back the water. We'll have a cup of tea.'

Georgiana glanced at the tea caddy. 'There's only a few leaves left, Dorrie.'

Dorrie tutted. 'Did you eat at all yesterday?'

'A bit.' Sighing, she nodded slightly, knowing she couldn't lie to Dorrie, who could ferret out a lie just by looking at you.

'A bit? You mean you gave whatever you had to Iris?' Dorrie eyed her like a displeased hospital matron. 'How can you feed a new baby if you don't eat?'

'I'll be fine once Roly comes home.'

'Oh, yes?' Dorrie huffed, lifting her large breasts up with one arm. 'And when does his lordship's boat dock? He's been gone two weeks and how that can be when he only goes up and down the Ouse to Hull and back is beyond me.'

'He sometimes goes further. He's been to London a few times, and Whitby. Last summer he went to Leith in Scotland. He brought us back some toffee, do you remember?'

'All I remember is you shining like the sun whenever he turns up and then is lost and dull again the minute his boat pulls up anchor. You and little Iris there are left to fend for yourselves for God only knows how long until Roly Carter decides to come home again.'

'He's a sailor.'

'He's a bloody boatman, Georgie, not a sailor in the navy. Sailors sail away to foreign countries. Your fella trots up and down the River Ouse like it's a pleasure outing.'

'That's not fair, Dorrie.' She felt the tears well.

They were interrupted by Danny bringing in the buckets and dumping them on the floor. 'I'm late now.'

'Get on with you. Stop your blathering and go to work,' his mother snapped. Dorrie set to making some tea and she also warmed the water to wash the baby.

Susan and Helen, Dorrie's daughters aged sixteen and fourteen, both came in and admired the baby.

'He's a beauty.' Susan smiled. She'd brought with her a pan of porridge left from their breakfast. 'I thought you might like some of this.' She ladled out a portion into two bowls, one for Georgiana and one for Iris.

Not to be left out, Posey, aged twelve, brought in Cissie, eight, and Angelina, the youngest at six.

'Where's Raymond?' Dorrie asked.

'Still in bed. He says he's not feeling well,' Posey answered, cooing at the baby. 'Pa said he'll watch him.'

'I'll be back shortly.' Dorrie left them, as they all knew Raymond was Dorrie's weak child and she was determined to nurture him to full health and adulthood. Unbelievably Dorrie had given birth to twelve children, and they'd all survived. Something she was terribly proud of and was to boast to anyone who'd listen. It was an achievement to be pleased about for a good percentage of babies rarely made it past their first birthday. Georgiana knew that first-hand as she'd given birth to a stillborn baby girl three years ago.

Eating the thin watery porridge, Georgiana watched the others fuss over the baby. She was tired, but the porridge was the first meal she'd eaten since she ate half a rotten apple yesterday morning and she was going to enjoy every mouthful.

She looked at Iris who was nibbling her spoonsful of porridge in the dainty way she had. Iris reminded her of her mother a great deal. Her mother, Henrietta Forsythe, a lady of social substance and breeding was petite and graceful, like a little bird, and Iris was so similar to her that it made Georgiana's heart ache. If only her family were different people, maybe she'd be living a different life now, but when her mother and her father had denounced her as their daughter for marrying beneath her class, a sobbing Georgiana had left home clinging to Roly and never returned.

'We'd best be getting off to work.' Susan smiled, pulling Helen behind her.

'Have a good day,' Georgiana called after them. The girls worked as housemaids at one of the hotels near the train station.

Dorrie returned and set to her task of washing the baby.

'How's Raymond?' Georgiana asked, feeling drowsy.

'It's his chest again. Wheezing like an old man, but I've daubed his chest with a poultice.'

'Take the coal back, Dorrie. Raymond needs a warm room.'

'And so do you and the babe. We have enough to share for now.' A flutter of worry crossed the other woman's face and she pushed back a tendril of greying hair from her face.

Georgiana glanced around the room, noticing the damp running down the walls, the dirty window set too high in the wall for easy cleaning. Holes in the skirting boards allowed mice and rats to come and go as they pleased, and the floorboards hadn't been washed in several months. Green and black mould spread like veins on the smoke-covered ceiling that was a mustard yellow shade. The room smelt dank and was as cold as ice even in summer. The only furniture they owned was the bed and a table with two chairs. It was all very different to the comfortable house she'd grown up in.

Was it any wonder Roly didn't want to come home and preferred to spend his days on the water in the fresh air?

'Can I walk with Cissie and Angelina to school by myself?' Iris asked in her quiet voice.

Nodding reluctantly for she always walked the girls to school, Georgiana reached over to pull the threadbare shawl over her daughter's thin shoulders. 'Hold Cissie's hand when crossing the roads.'

'Straight there and no dallying looking into shop windows,' Dorrie instructed.

Once the three little girls had gone from the room, Dorrie gave the washed and wrapped baby back to her and she nestled into the warmth of the bed and offered him a breast.

'He's sucking well,' Dorrie commented, tidying away. 'That's half the battle won.'

'What's wrong?' Georgiana asked, noticing Dorrie's paler than normal face.

With a thump, Dorrie sat on the chair. 'It's Raymond. He needs the doctor, but I've no money for it, or for the medicine he'll say I need to get for him.'

She reached over and held Dorrie's hand. 'If I had money, I'd give it to you.'

'I know you would, lass. My lads give up their wages, but I don't like asking all the time for them to do overtime.' Dorrie wiped a hand over her eyes. 'We get by, we have enough food and a roof over our heads, it's just Raymond needs constant medicine and who can afford to have the doctor on call day and night?'

'I understand the constant worry. I'm fretting about the rent. I don't have it. Roly has to come home before the week's out.'

'I have the rent, but I want to use it on Raymond, Sam won't hear of it. He says being thrown out for not paying the rent won't help Raymond.' Taking a deep breath, Dorrie launched herself up. 'Listen to me! Whining like an old hag.' She grinned. 'I'd best be off. I'm doing a shift behind Mrs Kemp's stall today while she attends a funeral.'

'I'll pop in and check on Raymond for you later.'

Dorrie smiled gratefully. 'Thanks, lass. Sam's home but he'll have his head in the newspaper all day before going to play cards at The Royal. Get some rest first though.'

Once Dorrie had gone and Frankie had finished feeding, Georgiana snuggled down in the mattress and pulled the blankets over them both. Tiredness overwhelmed her and she silently prayed Roly would come home today. How pleased he'd be to see he had a son.

She woke to loud knocking on the door. Frowning, she raised up onto one elbow, careful not to disturb Frankie. The knocking came again.

'Yes?'

The door opened and a workingman stood on the threshold, his cap in his hands.

'Mrs Carter?' he asked.

'Yes. Who are you?' She quivered it might be the rent man come early. God, how was she to put him off?

'Me name's Tim McDonald. I work at the timber yards on Skeldergate. I've come with news.'

'News?' She frowned in confusion. She didn't know anyone at the timber yard.

'Your husband, Roly Carter, the boat he works on docked at the yard this morning with some timber for us.'

'Roly?' She butted in. 'He's home?' Joy filled her.

The man twisted his cap in his fingers. 'You see, missus, there's been an accident.'

'An accident?' she repeated.

'Aye. Your husband has been hurt. He's been taken to the County Hospital. I were told to come and tell you.'

Her heart dropped. 'How badly injured is he?'

'I don't know, missus, sorry.'

'But he's not dead?' She barely got the words out.

'No, he was still alive when they took him away.'

'I must go to him.' She sat up straighter. Frankie made a murmur but nothing more.

'Right, well, I'll leave you to it. I've got to get back or I'll have my wages docked.'

'Thank you for coming to tell me.'

He pulled his cap on. 'Hope all goes well for you, missus.' He closed the door behind him.

She stood too quickly and swayed as a wave of dizziness flowed over her. She wore only her one remaining shift, but it had stains on it from giving birth no matter how careful she'd tried to not make a mess. Flinging it off, she quickly changed her undergarments, grabbed her corset which had seen better days and tied it on loosely, then donned a holey chemise and woollen petticoat. Lastly, from a nail in the wall, she took down her best and only skirt and a bodice of dark blue. The fine clothes she'd run away from home with had long been pawned for rent or food.

She pinned on her black felt hat and wrapped her black shawl about her shoulders before tucking Frankie inside it to protect him from the cold. She went next door and knocked.

'Come in,' Sam called from his chair by the window. 'Why, lass, what you are doing up?' he said as she entered the Turners' lodgings. Having been hurt in an accident at work himself five years ago, Sam only had one leg and had lost three fingers from his left hand. A scar ran down the left side of his face from temple to chin and at times he suffered severe headaches.

'Roly has been injured in an accident. He's in hospital. I need to go to him, Sam.'

'Nay, lass, you're not in any state to walk the streets. You've just had a bairn.'

'I've no choice.' She glanced at the sick boy on the trundle bed before the fire. 'How's Raymond?'

'Been sleeping. Can't get a thing down him, mind.' He looked worried. 'Dorrie will be home in an hour or two I should think.'

'I'd best go. If I'm not back by the time Iris comes home from school, can she sit in here with your girls?'

'Aye, of course she can.'

Georgiana hurried down the stairs to the bottom floor and out the wide double doors which had long been taken off by someone. The back of Birch House opened into a long narrow yard which in summer was festooned with drying washing but in winter harboured stray cats and dogs and rubbish.

Despite the low grey clouds and the chilly wind cutting between the buildings, Georgiana gingerly made her way out of the Bedern area of slum housing and along Goodramgate towards The County, as the hospital was shortened to by locals.

'Please don't let Roly be too badly injured,' she whispered to herself.

A light rain began to fall, adding to her miserable walk. She shivered when raindrops slipped off her hat and down her neck. Water was soon soaking through the holes in her boots, freezing her bare toes. She kept going, ignoring the aching in her sore body, the weight of the baby in her arms.

At the entrance to the hospital, she paused to catch her breath, but a sudden downpour sent her hurrying inside with the last of her energy.

A kind nurse came to her side. 'Can I help you?'

'Yes. My husband, Roly Carter, has been brought here. He was injured at work this morning.'

'Come and sit down and I'll make some inquiries.' The nurse led her to a bench similar to a church pew.

Grateful to sit down, Georgiana peeped at Frankie to check he wasn't wet, but he seemed warm enough.

For a time, she watched the comings and goings of the hospital staff and visitors. Everyone seemed intent on what they were doing and gave no heed to her sitting alone on the bench near the entrance. It felt like forever ago since she'd sat down. Frankie woke, squirming, wanting to be fed. Had the nurse forgotten about her?

About to rise and look for someone else to help her, she faltered on seeing the nurse return with a fierce looking man with spectacles.

'Mrs Carter?' he asked, indicating for her to remain seated.

'Yes.'

'I am Doctor Whittaker. I examined your husband when he was brought to us.'

'How is he?'

The doctor consulted his notes briefly, then sighed and stared directly at her. 'Your husband's injuries were extensive, Mrs Carter. He had received a heavy blow to his head, but it was his internal injuries which caused the fatal damage. There was nothing we could do… I am very sorry.'

'What do you mean?' Her head swam. The doctor's face came in and out of focus.

'Mrs Carter, I'm afraid your husband died shortly after his arrival here,' the doctor told her.

'No… please no.' She closed her eyes. *Oh, Roly. How could you leave me?*

'Nurse, perhaps take Mrs Carter somewhere quiet before she has to formally identify her husband.'

'Yes, Doctor.'

Dazed, Georgiana was led along a cold corridor and then another before the nurse ushered her into a long room lined in wood panelling and at the end held a large stained-glass window of Jesus. A gold cross stood on a dais.

'You may find some comfort in our chapel,' the nurse said, her eyes sad with sympathy. 'You can stay here for as long as you like. Then, when you're ready, I'll take you down to the morgue.'

Stunned, Georgiana couldn't think straight. Frankie whimpered but she couldn't tend to him such was her shock.

'Shall I take the baby for a little while? I'm due a break for ten minutes.' The nurse reached out her arms, kindness in her eyes.

Passing Frankie over left Georgiana feeling chilly where he'd been warm against her chest. It was that cold feeling that brought the tears dripping over her lashes.

Roly was dead. The man she'd run away from home for, defied her father for, was dead. He died the day their son was born. How was she to cope without him? To never see him smile at her again?

A tear tripped over her lashes and trickled down her cheek. Fear and panic overwhelmed her. She was a widow. Alone. The fate of her two children rested completely on her shoulders now. A shiver ran down her back. What was she going to do?

Chapter Two

Slipping off her silk evening gloves, Victoria Ashton sat at her dressing table. She yawned as she unclasped her emerald and diamond necklace, her most expensive and most beloved piece of jewellery, and laid it carefully in its case. Joseph had bought it for her on the birth of their first child, Kathleen, nine years ago. She wore it whenever she went to the theatre or to a special dinner or event, occasions which were becoming far too often for her liking, for socialising with the wealthy inhabitants of York had become a job all on its own. Yet a necessary one. The Ashton Home for Women and Children was a charity that would always need money while ever women and children of the city were being mistreated and in need. She and Joseph, with help from her best friends, Mercy and Harriet, had created a sanctuary for women needing shelter. For ten years they had strived together to create Victoria's dream into the success it was today.

The bedroom door opened, and Joseph walked in, looking tired and worn out. She rose and went into his arms, loving him more each day. First-hand, she'd seen the evidence of so many broken marriages, two people who at the beginning loved each other ended up with loathing in their eyes. However, she had been fortunate. Her marriage grew stronger as time went on. She adored Joseph as he did her. Together they shared four children, Kathleen Mercy, aged nine, Harriet Victoria, Ettie for short, aged seven and five-year-old Matthew Joseph.

'You look tired, my love,' she whispered, kissing him.

'And you look beautiful.' He smiled, standing back to admire her silk gown of forest green. 'Did you enjoy your evening at the theatre? Was it a success?'

'I did and we raised seventy-two pounds. Not a fortune but it will pay the coal bill for last quarter and go towards Christmas. And the play was particularly good value for money. Aunt Esther did herself proud organising it all for the benefit of us.'

'I wish I had attended it with you.'

'Hopefully you can next time. Are you hungry?'

Joseph sat on the blue velvet chaise longue at the end of their bed to take off his shoes. 'No, I ate at the hospital.'

'I'm pleased this is your last evening filling in for Doctor Harris. Working all day at our little hospital and then at the County is too much for you.' She turned her back to him so he could undo the many hooks on her bodice.

'Harris has done me good turns in the past. It was the least I could do while he was in London.' Finishing his task, he kissed her bare shoulder as she slipped the bodice off. 'I wrote to my parents asking them to come for Christmas.'

'Thank you. I should have done it weeks ago, but I'm so busy it kept slipping my mind.'

'Did the children behave tonight while you were out at the theatre?' Joseph asked, pulling off his tie.

'Yes, of course the children behaved, they dared not with Mercy.' She chuckled. Her best friend Mercy was a stickler for rules. 'They had their evening meal at Mercy's cottage and then read books until bedtime, Mercy told me when I stopped by her cottage to check on them.'

Joseph undid the buttons on his waistcoat. 'How is Harriet? Did she enjoy herself tonight?'

'She said she did,' Victoria answered, thinking of her other dear friend who she'd named her own daughter after. 'I believe she is relying on Jane more and more now in the shop.'

'Jane is quick and has aptitude,' he spoke of Mercy's eldest daughter. 'She can go further than working in Harriet's haberdashery. She could gain more education and become a teacher or something, a nurse, perhaps?'

'Jane doesn't want that, but I think Emily might.' Pulling on her nightgown, Victoria peered at Joseph where he lay reclined against the pillows. They treated Mercy's children no differently to their own. 'Emily wants to become a teacher. We should support her. She is very good in the schoolroom.'

'Then we shall do all we can to aid her in that profession, but she is only fourteen and may change her mind in a few years.'

Victoria brushed out her long hair, pondering on Emily's eagerness to be a teacher. Did it have something to do with Mr Nick Harlow, the new and rather handsome teacher they'd hired to teach the impoverished children who came to the gates with their mothers looking for shelter?

'Do you have any other plans for Mercy's children or our own?' Joseph joked.

She climbed into bed and playfully slapped his shoulder. 'I want them all to be happy.'

'They are happy. Do not fret.' He kissed her and gazed into her eyes. 'Forget everyone for a little while. It's just you and me, my love.'

She snuggled into his arms. 'Have I told you how much I adore you, Doctor Ashton?'

He rained kisses over her face, down her neck and at the tender spot behind her ear. 'Maybe you have, but remind me…'

She chuckled and held him tight, silently thanking the fates that brought them together years ago.

The next morning after breakfast with the children, Victoria left the house and walked the path to the small white iron gate set in a tall wall. This was the boundary between her private world and that of the Home. When designing the estate, Joseph had insisted that they set their double-storey house and Mercy's cottage within its own acre walled boundary, giving them privacy and also security.

The extensive buildings and gardens of the women's home were spread across four acres out of the five that Victoria had been bequeathed by her late Uncle Harold, a successful banker in York. His legacy had helped create the much needed home, which comprised of a large three-storey main building built of red brick, an attached hospital which was Joseph's domain, and service outbuildings. Vegetable gardens supplied the whole estate and offered the chance for mothers and their children to learn about food and how to grow it. Victoria firmly believed education was learnt inside and outside of the classroom.

Crossing the gardens, Victoria waved to Mr Nevis, the head gardener, who even at this early time of the morning had a small group of children helping him cultivate garden beds for spring planting. Another group of children could be seen in the glasshouse tending to the winter vegetables with Robbie, the garden labourer. The hens and ducks had been let out and were scratching around the gardens.

Entering the main building, Victoria heard the noise of voices coming from the dining hall, where mothers and children ate their meals. Usually, she would go in and say good morning to everyone, but today she had a full list of tasks that would keep her occupied until late.

Her office was at the front of the building, a large square room painted yellow with white trim. It was a room she had made to look professional but also comfortable. A small seating area was placed by the large window overlooking the front entrance. The fireplace shone with black leading and the tiles surrounding it where tastefully decorated with delicate flowers. Her wide desk of walnut matched the bookcase along one wall. Jugs and vases of greenhouse flowers stood on the mantlepiece and the two occasional tables near the blue damask sofa. This room was the hub of the entire estate. From her desk she ran the home as well as any prime minister ran the country. Just as the prime minster had his aides, Victoria had her helpers. Mercy was her second in charge and without her, Victoria knew she'd have struggled in the early days as Joseph worked long hours at the hospital.

The home had a board of governors consisting of Joseph, Mercy, Harriet, Victoria's aunt, Esther Dobson, Doctor Harris and Victoria as chairwoman. Being a charity, Victoria and Mercy worked hard to bolster their finances. Ongoing fundraising took energy and strategy, but Victoria was determined to never turn away a woman in need, though sometimes that meant finding extra beds and food.

In the beginning, they'd planned for fifty women and their children. Naturally, it didn't always turn out to be that number. Sometimes, the number of women and children needing assistance and shelter could drop slightly, but mostly the numbers swelled to seventy or more, which provided some attention to detail as Victoria and Mercy allocated more beds in the dorms and chairs at tables in the dining room. But no one was ever turned away. That was the Ashtons' policy.

While within the home, the women where not only provided with shelter, clean clothes and food, but also the chance to turn their lives around. They were offered skills to learn, cooking, sewing, household management as well as learning to read and write alongside their children. Victoria and Mercy aided them in finding suitable work, and when they had saved some of their wages, helped to find them safe accommodation. Each woman who left the home to set up her new life was given full support. Victoria made sure they had delivery of coal and produce for the first month and she or Mercy would visit them weekly. Joseph provided free health care.

Not all the women were grateful or happy to better themselves. Many cases refused to change and would return to the slums, back to the abuse, the filth and squalor, endangering not only their lives but those of their children.

In the last ten years, Victoria had lost count of how many times they'd sent for the police when a husband would turn up demanding his family back, or a drunken father would threaten to kill a fallen daughter. The highs and lows of running a home for unfortunate women took its toll on occasion, but Victoria could never turn her back on it. Those women and children needed aid and she would provide it as best she could.

Mercy knocked briefly and entered carrying a small tray containing the first post. 'I'm off into town shortly. Did you want me to do anything for you?'

'I need to go into town myself, but later. I'm to visit the tenement in Skinner's Yard in Walmgate to see if any rooms are suitable for us to let. Mrs Banks is not adjusting to living here. She is fighting with the other mothers in her dorm. If we can rent a room for her, it will solve a few problems.'

'Mrs Banks is ungrateful. We offer her a roof and food for her and her children and she repays us with abuse and her wayward and rude children disrupt everyone else.'

'Luckily, for every Mrs Banks we receive, we find ten lovely ladies who cause no trouble and who are appreciative of our help.'

'Do you want me to come with you to Walmgate?' Sitting in the chair opposite the desk, Mercy flipped through the mail, sorting it out into different piles.

'Do you have time? Joseph was to come with me but he's catching up on work at our hospital after all the time he's spent at the County lately.'

'I can make time and it'll be grand to have Joseph back with us full time. I want him to take a look at little Will Taylor's finger. It's infected. Oh, and Jill Moore is due for her baby any day, the woman is massive. Did you notice Peggy Alcock's limp isn't getting any better? Her husband should be in jail for the thrashing he gave her. His steel-capped boots did so much damage to poor Peggy's body, never mind the baby she lost. I'm glad he's done a runner. I hope he never returns to York because she'll go back to him, I know it.' Mercy's look of disgust was exactly how Victoria felt, but they knew they couldn't stand in the way of the women they gave aid to and if those bashed and battered wives returned to their husbands there was nothing Victoria or Mercy could do but support them and hope their lives changed for the better.

'I'm sure Joseph will see to them all. I know he's worried about the Draper baby, who is not putting on weight.' Victoria read through her diary. 'Before you go, we need to discuss the Christmas dinner. Shall we do the same as last year and have a midday meal and a concert in the evening or change it to a later meal and some entertainment during the day?'

'The concert was good last year but the children did become tired at the end. It went on for far too long.'

'That's because everyone wanted a turn at performing, whether they were good or not.' Victoria grinned. 'Remember Mrs Hughes and her bird warbling?'

'Lord, how could I forget.' Mercy giggled. 'And what about that young woman we had staying with us, Fiona, wasn't it? She spent five minutes dancing out of time to Joseph on the piano.'

'The children forgot their words when it was their turn to sing carols.'

Mercy laughed. 'And I spent so many hours teaching them!'

'It was a fun but exhausting night.' Victoria smiled fondly at the memories.

'Shall we have a concert every *second* year then? It'll give us time to forget the previous one.' Mercy chuckled, opening one envelope, then she grimaced. 'The cobbler's bill.'

'Add it to the other bills. I'll be paying them all today. It might drain the coffers for a while, but I hate the thought of being in any debt over Christmas.'

'There's always debt. We've not paid off the loan for building this place yet.'

'No, but I can manage that one.' Victoria took out a ledger from her desk drawer. 'It's the smaller bills I want done with and out of the way. Besides, the merchants we use should be paid timely to give them a good Christmas, too.'

'So, what shall we do this Christmas then?' Mercy asked. 'We can take the children carolling on Christmas Eve, attend church on Christmas morning…'

Victoria thought to a conversation she had with Joseph a few weeks ago. 'I'm thinking we have the main celebration on Christmas Eve, then you and I can be free to have Christmas Day with just our family.'

Mercy's eyebrows rose. 'That will be a first. Has Joseph finally worn you down about it?'

'He mentions it every year.'

'Who can blame him? He wants a family Christmas in the cottage without all the women and children about.'

'I do enjoy having the Christmas meal at midday with the women and children, but I think this year we do it on Christmas Eve. Then perhaps we can organise some games in the afternoon? We will have Christmas Day just with ourselves in the cottage and then on Boxing Day we could take all the children skating on the duck pond at Mr Dartman's Farm? I'm sure he'll let us if we ask him.'

'We don't have enough skates for everyone. We've only ten pairs.'

'They can take it in turns. It'll only be the bigger children skating.'

'Right well, that seems a good idea. I'll inform Mrs Shelton what we'll be doing, and she can begin planning and ordering the food. She'll want to take on extra staff in the kitchen for such a busy week.'

Victoria nodded. 'Yes, that's fine.'

'I did want to talk to you about the laundry duties.' Mercy sighed. 'You know Agnes is struggling?'

Frowning, Victoria gave Mercy her full attention. Agnes was their head laundress, an older woman who had nowhere to live when she arrived at the gates five years ago, gaunt and penniless. For her bread and board, she ran the laundry house and the situation had been perfect until recently when she began to have health problems. 'We have employed three more girls to help Agnes in the laundry as well as the women helping out when they can. Are those girls not up to scratch?'

'Not really. Daphne and her sister have not turned up for work for the last two days. Agnes is furious. It puts more work on the mothers staying here to help out, but we have too many women in poor health who are beyond the strenuous task of laundry work.'

'Then let us hire some more girls.' Victoria wrote notes in her diary.

A knock on the door preceded Kathleen, Victoria's oldest daughter, and who was named after Victoria's dear Irish friend who'd befriended her when Victoria had fallen on hard times and was shunned by her family. Victoria was still haunted by dreams of Kathleen dying in the floods that swallowed their dwellings in the slums.

At nine years old, Kathleen was a pretty girl with the same copper hair as her mother and a happy disposition of a young girl who was loved by her family and lived a life. 'Mama, Mr Harlow hasn't come into class.'

Victoria glanced at the clock. It was past eight thirty, the time when Mr Harlow began teaching the children in the schoolroom next to the dining hall. She rose and headed out of her office. 'I'm sure he's simply been caught up by something.'

Heading for the dining hall with Mercy and Kathleen following, Victoria kept a lid on her annoyance at the handsome teacher she'd employed. Educating the children was part of the Home's policy and Mr Harlow had come with good qualifications and a winning smile. He had all the staff at the home eating out of his hand, something which amused Victoria at first. But lately he'd become a little sloppy in his duties. She often caught him out of class and chatting to the mothers with small babies, or with the single women staff. His good looks and easy manner made him a firm favourite in an institution largely populated by females.

The dining room was empty, the tables cleared from breakfast. Victoria walked along to the communal sitting room, a large space with a fireplace and comfy sofas. The walls were lined with books and boxes of toys were piled in the corners. It was the main area for all the inhabitants of the home to relax and socialise.

A few mothers and their small children were sat in the room, the mothers knitting and chatting, while babies slept in prams or cradles by the windows and toddlers played with coloured blocks of wood, dolls and stuffed bears.

'Good morning, ladies,' Victoria greeted them as one. 'Has anyone seen Mr Harlow this morning?'

One woman, Jessie, who'd been at the home for two weeks as she waited to be rehomed, looked up from her knitting. 'He didn't come down for breakfast.'

Victoria turned to Mercy. 'Will you look around outside? I'll go up to his room. Kathleen, go to the schoolroom and ask Emily to read to the children.'

Climbing the main staircase, Victoria nodded and smiled to the mothers she passed. Up here the two dormitory rooms held the sleeping quarters of all the women and their children. But built up in the attics was extra bedrooms, storage rooms and at the far end was the two rooms allocated to Mr Harlow.

Victoria knocked sharply on the door and waited. No noise came from the other side. Perturbed, she tried the handle, but it was locked. Annoyed with herself for not thinking to bring her master set of keys, she knocked again. Still no answer.

Irritated, she marched back downstair to her office and took her keys from the drawer. She once again mounted the stairs. She didn't have time for any of this.

'Mrs Ashton?' A woman called to her from the landing, holding a newborn baby to her chest.

'Yes, Phyllis?' She paused at the bottom of the narrow staircase leading up to the attics.

'I've received a letter this morning.' The young girl, no more than sixteen, looked uncertain. 'Do you think it's from my grandmother in Edinburgh?'

Knowing Phyllis couldn't read or write, Victoria took the letter she held out. Three weeks ago, Phyllis had been found one dark night behind the laundry in labour. The girl had been thrown out of home by her father and left to fend for herself. Victoria had taken her in and assisted Joseph in delivering the baby. Since that night, the poor girl had been in a state of depression and worry about her future. Phyllis had spoken of her grandmother who lived in Edinburgh and asked Victoria to write to her to see if she would take her in.

Reading the short note, Victoria smiled in relief. 'Yes, it's from your grandmother, Gloria Hind. She says she was happy to receive your letter and is saddened by your situation.'

'Will she not have me then?' Phyllis butted in.

'Let me see…' She read the last few lines. 'Your grandmother writes that if you can get the fare to Edinburgh, you can live with her.'

'And the baby?'

'She doesn't mention the baby,' Victoria stated sadly. 'That doesn't mean the baby isn't included in the invitation.'

Phyllis gazed down at the tiny infant swaddled in a white blanket. 'I'm not giving her up. She's mine.'

'No one is asking you to give her up. Do you want to live with your grandmother? You don't have to. You can stay here longer.'

'I would like to be with family, if you don't mind me saying so. This place is nice and all, but it's not… the women are not my family…'

Victoria patted her shoulder. 'I perfectly understand. We will buy your train fare to Edinburgh.'

'You will?' Phyllis's eyes widened in surprise and then filled with tears. 'Oh, thank you, Mrs Ashton. No one has ever been as kind to me as you have been. You're a saint.'

'Hardly a saint. Go and have a cup of tea and I'll come and find you in a little while and we'll sort out your leaving plans.'

Carrying on up the staircase, Victoria knocked again on Mr Harlow's door. With no response she found the correct key on the ring and unlocked the door. She'd not been into this small sitting room since Mr Harlow moved in and was at once assailed by the stuffiness and stale odour. All around the room were debris of the man's habits. Half-empty snuff boxes lay disregarded on tables, numerous wine bottles, opened books and newspapers littered the floor. Hanging off the open bedroom door was shirts and towels.

'Mr Harlow?' Incensed at the mess, Victoria stormed into the bedroom only to stop short on seeing the teacher passed out with his arms around a naked woman in bed. 'Mr Harlow!' she shouted.

The woman jumped up with a scream and quickly covered herself.

'Mrs Lesley.' Victoria fumed that one of the women she'd saved had given herself to the teacher. 'This Home is not for wanton women! Get yourself dressed and downstairs to my office.'

'I can explain.'

'Your actions are explanation enough. Just go.'

Harlow murmured then moved one leg but didn't wake up. The room stank of wine. She flung opened the curtains and a weak stream of winter light brightened the room showcasing the clutter of it.

Victoria nudged Harlow roughly in the shoulder. 'Get up!'

He groaned and rolled over, the sheet slipping down his chest. 'Leave me alone.'

Reaching for the water jug, in one quick movement she threw it over him.

'What the bloody hell!' Harlow jerked upright, wiping the water dripping from his bloodshot eyes.

'I could ask you the same question, sir?' she sneered through tight lips. 'You know the rules of no fraternising with the women. You are dismissed immediately. I'll give you an hour to pack your things and leave.'

'Mrs Aston, please, let me explain.'

'As I just mentioned to Mrs Lesley, your actions are explanation enough. One hour or I'll call the constable.' She stormed from the room, angrier than she'd been in a very long time.

Mr Harlow, when he first arrived, showed such skills in dealing with children from the backstreet slums who were abused and neglected. He became a figure to them that ensued trust and authority. From him the children enjoyed learning. He was young and encouraging, one to bend the rules and not rule with a willow stick on hands and backsides. His modern approach to teaching and learning gave Victoria such a sense of happiness that the children she housed would have not only a roof over their heads and food, but an education to better themselves, to maybe break the cycle they'd been born into.

Now she felt foolish for giving into his charming ways and his lyrical prose on *new and enlightening teaching*. He'd conned her, obviously and only wanted to dally with the women in her care.

Furious, she'd now have to find the time to search for a new teacher, put advertisements in the newspapers, sort through the applicants and conduct interviews, and all before Christmas.

In her office, Mrs Lesley stood by the window staring out, her hair tied in a ragged bun, her clothes dishevelled. A sorry sight indeed. She watched Victoria take her seat behind the desk before slowly walking over to her. 'I'm sorry, Mrs Ashton.'

'For which bit? Your conduct or being caught out?' Victoria spoke harshly, full of disappointment. 'I do not run a prison, Mrs Lesley. All the women who come here have the freedom of this building and can come and go from the grounds as they please, within reason. We have few rules here, but one rule is that once you are living here no men are to be entertained. It is a rule to keep the vulnerable safe. Mr Harlow had an important position here and was trusted. He has broken that trust, as have you.'

'Please don't send me away.' The woman was only twenty-five but looked ten years older.

'And why should you stay? You obviously don't care to live under our rules. Why should you have a bed here when there are others out there in need of it?'

'I have nowhere else to go.'

'Perhaps you should have thought of that before you went to Mr Harlow's room?' Victoria snapped.

Mrs Lesley wrung her hands together. 'You took me in when my husband run off with another woman. I had no place left to go. I have no family, no friends to take me in. If you throw me out, I'll end up in the workhouse, or worse, a brothel.'

'If my memory serves me right, you've been with us for six weeks. In that time have you been looking for positions?'

'Mercy, I mean Mrs Felling, has been helping me apply for jobs but without a proper work reference only the character reference that you provide, I've not been taken on.' Mrs Lesley didn't meet Victoria's eyes.

'Is that the truth?' Victoria didn't believe her. A character reference from her and Mercy was enough to get the women who've left here a position in a variety of work as has been proven for the last ten years.

'Aye, it's the truth.'

'Who did you last apply to?'

'Um… I can't remember…' Mrs Lesley took a step back. 'Listen, it's probably best if I go now.'

'You just said you wanted to stay.'

'I don't belong here…' Mrs Lesley backed away.

'You've been offered work and turned it down, haven't you?' Victoria had dealt with so many different women over the years. Women from all walks of life, women who were shy, grateful, nasty, belligerent, helpful, mentally unstable, nervous, funny, eager to help or plain lazy. She'd met them all and this had given her an instinct to read people.

'One job, that's all. It weren't right for me,' Mrs Lesley defended.

‘No?’

‘No. I didn’t want to work in Rowntree’s chocolate factory. I had a cousin who worked there, and she hated it.’

‘A cousin?’ Victoria instantly noticed the slip. ‘When you came here you told us you had no family at all.’

Mrs Lesley’s hands fidgeted. ‘Aye, well, she’s a distant cousin, we don’t talk. We fell out years ago.’

Victoria opened her drawer and took out a tin box which she unlocked with a key. She counted out twenty shillings and slid them across the desk towards Mrs Lesley. Then taking a ledger from the corner of her desk she wrote in it and asked Mrs Lesley to sign her name or make her mark. The woman managed to write in shaky form her name.

Victoria looked at the other woman. ‘Twenty shillings to see you on your way and you have two character references from myself and Mrs Felling. Mrs Shelton will make you up a food hamper to take with you. I wish you well in your life, Mrs Lesley.’

Grabbing the coins, the young woman stared at her for a long moment. Then with a shrug, she turned and stomped out of the office.

Bowing her head, Victoria let out a sigh, but a knock on the door straightened her again. ‘Come in.’

Mr Harlow walked in. Dressed neatly in a dark suit with his hair freshly combed, he looked presentable except for his bloodshot eyes. He placed his suitcase at his feet and held a hat in his hand. ‘Mrs Ashton.’

‘I hope it was worth it, Mr Harlow?’

‘Not at all. My embarrassment is overwhelming, but my self-loathing at letting you down is complete. I am ashamed to have fallen so low and abused the valuable position you so generously gave me.’

‘You have. My disappointment is great indeed.’ Once more she counted money out from the tin and placed it on the desk and then wrote in the ledger. ‘Your wages owing for this quarter up to the Christmas break.’

'That is most charitable of you.'

'It is.'

He stepped forward and took the money. 'If I should gain another position and they write to you for a reference?'

'I shall think about it. I do not wish to see anyone out of work, Mr Harlow, but nor will I lie for you. You have a drinking problem I suspect from the amount of wine bottles in your room and a complete disregard to those who help you. We gave you a chance, Mr Harlow, a chance to teach in your modern way. Not many schools will do that. Had you conducted yourself with more respect, you could have lived here for many years and given a great service to the children who enter our establishment.'

He bowed. 'There is nothing for me to say. You are correct. I ruined a superb chance to teach my own way.' His handsome face showed his unhappiness. 'I am weak, Mrs Ashton.'

'At this Home we *help* the weak, Mr Harlow. Therefore, *we* cannot be weak ourselves. Good day.' She dismissed him. A headache was building behind her eyes.

As he left Emily came in, close to tears as she stared first at Mr Harlow and then at Victoria. 'Aunt Victoria? Is it true? Mr Harlow is leaving?'

'It is.' She waited for Mr Harlow to close the door behind him. 'Emily, dearest, can you run the schoolroom, please? Just for this week. Kathleen will help you.'

'But Mr Harlow was so good.' A tear trickled down her face, a younger version of her mother. 'We all liked him so much.'

'Yes, but he has behaved badly and had to be dismissed.'

'I'm sure he didn't mean to?'

Victoria could have smiled at her naivety. 'Unfortunately, Mr Harlow must go. It is done.'

'But Aunt…'

'Enough, Emily. He is gone. We must do our best until I find a replacement.'

Emily ran out of the room crying and it confirmed to Victoria that her suspicions were correct. Emily was infatuated with Mr Harlow, and it was perhaps a good thing the handsome teacher would no longer be around.

When the door opened again, Victoria groaned out loud. She closed her eyes at the thought of any more problems. Her head was really pounding now.

'Darling?' Joseph's voice was a little anxious.

She stood and went into his arms, needing his comfort. 'It's not even midday and I'm done.'

'You work too hard.' He kissed the top of her head where she nestled on his shoulder.

She leaned back to grin at him. 'Says the doctor who barely sleeps.'

'I'm hearing rumours of Mr Harlow and Mrs Lesley?'

'I've sent them both away. I caught them in bed.'

Joseph led her to the sofa by the fireplace. Seated together she told him about the morning's events.

'What was the man thinking?' Joseph shook his head.

'We both know what he was thinking,' Victoria scoffed.

'The stupid fool. He's lost a good position and a roof over his head.' Joseph added more coal to the fire. 'I can't say I'm surprised really. I always thought him arrogant, a charmer.'

'Yes, but he was good with the children. Teaching and encouraging twenty odd children of all ages and from desperate backgrounds is a skill. Under his guidance they were happy to go to the schoolroom each morning. He will be difficult to replace.'

'You will find someone. But perhaps engage a female though this time?' Joseph grinned.

She gave him a sour look. 'You're not funny.'

'Maybe not,' he kissed her lovingly, 'but I have other talents…'

'It's the middle of the day…' She half-heartedly protested as he deepened the kiss.

'A man is allowed to kiss his wife,' he murmured against her lips.

A knock on the door broke them apart.

Joseph stood with a sigh. 'Promise me that at Christmas we'll have some time alone, just you and me. Even if it's just a walk. I would very much enjoy a few precious hours with my wife alone and when we aren't both too tired to do anything but sleep. Can we have that?'

She rose and cupped his cheek. 'We will, darling. I promise.'

He gazed into her eyes. 'I'm holding you to it, Victoria.'

The knock came again, and Joseph left to open the door and leave the room.

Victoria hoped she could keep the promise as Robbie the undergardener brought in a bucketful of coal and behind him Mercy entered carrying her notebook. In the corridor was a gaggle of women waiting to speak to her, no doubt about Mr Harlow, and somewhere a baby was crying loudly.

Her head continued to pound.

Chapter Three

In the biting cold wind, Ruthie Benson struggled along Walmgate in the dark, holding her thin shawl around her shoulders with one hand while with the other she gripped tightly to the warm meat pie she'd just bought for her brother's supper. Gerald would be home from the brewery where he worked by six o'clock and it was already gone half past five. She quickened her steps. She'd be in for it if she was home after him. He didn't care that she had to walk the length of York from where she worked as a housemaid in a grand house on Bootham to their shabby two rooms in the slums of Walmgate.

Since being taken on as a scullery maid three years ago, she'd worked her way up to being a housemaid, which came with a live-in option but Gerald had refused to allow her to move away from him. She could only keep her job if she came home every night after her shift and that meant waking up at four each morning and trudging the streets in all weathers to Bootham on the other side of the city and then repeat the journey after a long day on her feet.

Yet, despite the long tiring days, she wouldn't give up the position. Working for the Coledale family gave her a respite from the drudgery of the tenements, the filth and the poverty. In the Coledale house she was surrounded by clean rooms decorated beautifully and furnished with the best pieces money could buy. As a servant of the Coledale family, she was given two uniforms a year, three aprons and cuff sets, a half day off every second week and a full weekend off every three months. Also included was breakfast and a midday meal – the only food she ate.

Ruthie cherished her job and wouldn't give it up no matter how many times Gerald demanded she did. He wanted her home to care for him and their rooms. Though if she did that how he'd cope without her money, she didn't know. Her wages were his and he gave her only a small amount back to buy food. As the oldest and the man of the family, he declared it was his responsibility to take control of her money, which included using it to buy beer each night. That he sometimes spent it all and didn't pay the rent was something she couldn't speak about. Confronting her brother about anything usually ended up with her sporting an injury from his brutal fists.

Although late into the afternoon, the banging and clanging from the iron foundry filled the air. Noise also came from the brewery, the timber yard, the slaughterhouse and a number of other industries squashed into such a small area. There was no peace from the booming sounds until the whistle blew at seven and the men downed tools and went home. Turning left, Ruthie entered Hurst's Yard, a mean filthy space bordered on both sides by overcrowded tenement buildings housing mainly the poor and desperate Irish escaping the famine back home in Ireland.

She hated this area. Her brother had made them come into the city when their parents died five years ago from fever. Ruthie had been fourteen and her world had been turned upside down. The little cottage they'd lived in on the outskirts of the city was taken from them when Gerald didn't pay the rent and so they'd gathered their few belongings and walked into the city centre to find work and lodgings.

For a year they lived on the floor of one of Gerald's friend's house before he and Gerald argued, and they were kicked out.

They slept rough for a few weeks in church doorways, under bridges, anywhere they could find some form of shelter. Eventually, Gerald found a job at the brewery, and they were told about the filthy two rooms in Hurst's Yard.

Ruthie had vowed never to be homeless again and worked hard to better herself. At fifteen she went to a nearby church's Sunday school and begged to be taught her letters. Within six months she was able to take a character reference from the reverend and applied for housemaid positions. Gaining employment with the Coledale family turned her life around somewhat, and she became a little happier working in a nice house for a decent family. However, Gerald became only angrier at the injustices of their life. Working long hours for minimal pay, living in one of the worst parts of York and never having anything pleasant created a monster in her brother. Gerald became a heavy drinker, a fighter, a tormentor and her jailor.

Side-stepping the piles of rubbish the wind swirled into mounds along the dark yard, Ruthie entered the crumbling building and went up the rickety staircase to the floor above. Using the key on the string around her neck, and with no light in the stairwell, she fumbled about until the key fitted into the lock and opened the door.

She paused slightly to glance up at the floor above, but although there was plenty of noise from the other inhabitants, no light shone, no special person was waiting for her to come home. Micky O'Dowd was her special someone. The cheeky Irish lad who lived above with his family. The blue-eyed sweet-talking young man who promised to take her away from Gerald and York as soon as he'd saved enough money. She loved him and he loved her. They would be married soon, hopefully, and she couldn't wait to be Mrs O'Dowd.

Micky worked on the trains and was gone for days sometimes. She was lucky if they got together once a week, and only when their shifts allowed, and Gerald was away from the yard. But for the last eight months she and Micky had an understanding. They kept it quiet, obviously because of Gerald, and how he'd react. He didn't like the Irish upstairs, or any Irish come to that. He said they came over here in droves and took all the jobs. Well, she loved the Irish, especially Micky, and one day they'd be married and gone from this scummy place, and Gerald would have no control over her then.

Sighing in disappointment that Micky wasn't waiting for her, Ruthie entered the freezing room. She was carefully not to knock over the bucket by the door which caught the drips from the floor above where something leaked through the ceiling, creating a stain that spread a little more each day. Dust from cracked plaster floated gently onto the floor as she shut the door.

The fire was out, and she quickly put a match to the screwed newspaper and broken slithers of wood gathered from roaming streets searching for ruined crates. There were a few pieces of coal in the bottom of the bucket. Not enough to last the night but it would do to give the room some warmth this evening. Hopefully, Gerald would bring a bag of coal home.

She closed the little door on the range and sat the pie on the top plate to keep warm. Within half an hour she'd filled two buckets of water from the pump at the end of the yard and had a wash. The room held only a chair, a stool and Gerald's iron bed in the corner. The other small room off to the right was her little bedroom which held only a bed. Her few clothes were hung on nails in the wall. There was nothing pretty in the place, no comfort. They didn't have the money spare for nice things. Her wages went on coal and ale, and the small amount of money Gerald gave her, when he remembered, she bought his food. His wage was to pay the rent, but mostly it went on ale and the rent man came and left with demands of back rent and threats of eviction.

The kettle was boiling ready for a cup of tea. She was hungry and thirsty but knew better than to nibble at the edge of the pie or even pour a cup of tea without Gerald's permission.

If he came home to find her sitting and having a cup of tea, he'd knock her block off and no mistake.

Singing came from beyond the door. The O'Dowd and Finnigan families upstairs where great ones for singing. Sometimes they sing happy Irish tunes and at other times sad laments that tore at the soul.

A tiny knock and a head popped in. Tina O'Dowd, Micky's little sister, edged half her body in as though unsure if she could enter.

'Tina?' Ruthie smiled, encouraging her.

'I'm to tell you that Micky's gone away. He said for me to tell you.'

'For how long?'

The thin girl, wearing a dirty threadbare dress, shrugged. 'He's gone home.'

'Home?'

'Aye.'

'To Ireland?'

'Aye. To visit the old folk with Mammy.' Then she promptly closed the door.

Devasted, Ruthie wrapped her arms about herself. Micky gone. That wasn't what she'd been expecting. Micky gave her some hope that soon she'd be gone from Hurst's Yard. She loved him. He said he'd keep her safe from Gerald, but first he had to save some money. That's what he said to her only last week. She believed him. Lord, how she believed him.

She nervously laid her hand over the small swell of her stomach. She might not have a mother to give her advice, but she'd lived cheek by jowl with people long enough to know about the facts of life. What she and Micky did on occasion, the wonderful times when he'd take her willing body and whisper how much she meant to him, had begun to grow another life.

Ruthie huddled before the fire as the church bells tolled seven times. Gerald was late, which meant he was drinking. Hands shaking, Ruthie poured a cup of weak tea with no sugar or milk. Her eyes strayed to her stomach again, hidden in the folds of her coat. It was easy to hide the little bump under coat at home for the rooms were always freezing, but her skirts at work were becoming tighter. How much longer could she hold out? How long was Micky going to be away?

She heard footsteps on the stairs and rushed to the door hoping it was one of the O'Dowd's. Peeking out, she smiled at Niamh O'Dowd, Micky's sister.

'How do, Ruthie,' Niamh said passing by, carrying an empty basket.

'Niamh, has Micky truly gone back to Ireland?'

The young woman turned back. 'Aye, with Mammy. The old folk sent word that they are being rehoused and Mammy needed to go and see what's going on. Micky went with her to help.'

'When will he be back?'

Niamh grinned, her blue eyes so like Micky's flashing in amusement. 'I knew you two had something going on. You keen on my brother are you, pet?'

'Yes, but my brother must never know.'

Niamh's pretty face fell. 'No, he's a miserable bugger is your Gerald. He'll not hear it from me.'

'Thanks.'

'Micky and Mammy won't be back in York for weeks, maybe a month or so. He should've told you.'

'We don't always see each other every day with our work.'

'Well, he'll be back before you know it. Ta-ra.' She gave a nod and carried on down the stairs.

Closing the door, Ruthie leaned her head against it. A month. She could hold out for a month. She had to, there was no other choice.

Sitting by the fire, she kept the flames going, adding bits of the precious coal. Her stomach grumbled with hunger as the church bells rang out eight times. She'd last eaten at one o'clock, seven hours ago. She made a cup of tea from the lukewarm kettle, then impulsively cut a slice of the meat pie that was no longer hot.

'Bugger Gerald,' she muttered defiantly. She'd eat the pie and then go to bed.

Noise on the landing lifted her head as she bit into the juicy meat and gravy. The door burst opened as flakes of pastry floated down from her mouth.

Gerald lumbered in, swaying, cursing as he tripped over the bucket catching the drips and sent it flying. 'Christ's sake!' He straightened, focused on staying upright and then peered at Ruthie by the fire. 'What the bloody hell are you doing?'

Heart pounding, she swallowed. 'I've been waiting for hours for you to come home. Where have you been?'

'None of your damn business, that's for sure.' He staggered over to the stool in front of the fire, knocking her out of the way. Her brother was a large man, like their father had been, but where their father had been jovial and kind, Gerald was nasty and mean.

'You're drunk. Wasting good money on ale!' she accused, hating him.

'I'll do what I like with my money.'

'Then don't blame me when we have no food or coal. My wages don't stretch far enough, you know that.'

'Who do you think you are nagging at me like a fishwife!' His small dark eyes found the pie. 'You've eaten my food.'

'It's mine as well!'

'You eat at that fancy house you work at. No doubt stuffing your face all day while I'm slaving at the brewery!'

'Hardly stuffing my face.'

His hand lashed out at her head before she was aware of it, knocking her backwards on the chair. 'Make me some tea,' he snarled, grabbing the pie with both hands and stuffing it into his face without thought to a plate or knife and fork.

'You disgust me!' Crying, Ruthie ignored the pain throbbing at the side of her head and set about raking the embers to get enough heat to if not boil the kettle, then at least make it warmer than it was.

'Where's the coal?' Gerald mumbled between mouthfuls.

'All gone. You were meant to bring some home.'

'And how am I to do that?' he snapped, eyes narrowed with hostility. 'Am I made of bloody money?'

'You've been paid today.' She didn't look at him and prayed that he'd not put all his wage over the bar.

'I've no money for coal. You'll have to nick some.'

'I ain't.' Ruthie straightened, the tea forgotten. 'I'm off to bed.'

Gerald jerked to his feet, dropping the last bit of pie crust to the floor. He grabbed her wrist, yanking her back. 'You'll do as I say. Get out there now and go find some coal or wood or anything to warm this bloody place up. It's like coming home to a morgue.'

'It's after eight, Gerald. I'm not traipsing around the streets in the freezing night to find firewood.'

'You'll do as you're bloody told, bitch.' His fist hit her jaw so hard her head snapped back with a crack.

Stars darted before her eyes, the pain ricocheting around her body. She crumbled to her knees as he hit her again. 'Stop! Stop. You'll mark me!' Her thoughts were of losing her job. She couldn't work at the Coledale house with a bruised face. Before when Gerald hit her, it was always on the body or slaps to the head where she displayed no sign of his beatings. If she was tender and sore at work no one would ever know.

He pushed her away from him, cursing violently. He lifted a leg to kick her as she lay on the floor, but she curled into a ball instinctively to protect the small life she carried.

'No more, Gerald!' she screamed at him.

He hesitated and then slumped onto the chair. 'Get out of my sight.'

The pain made her light-headed as she slowly made her way into the next room. Her bedroom was nothing more than a box room with a squeaky iron bed covered with two worn blankets full of holes. She climbed into bed, tears falling silently. Micky had to come back soon.

Chapter Four

As the snow floated gently down, Georgiana walked the cobbled streets. She'd been going into shops, asking for work, but with no references, she was turned away each time. For three weeks she'd been a widow, yet it felt far longer. Roly's boss had given her some money, enough to pay the rent for a month, but that was all she had, and the month was nearly up. Good-hearted neighbours like Dorrie gave her food, but such charity couldn't continue. Working was her only way forward.

Only, how was she to work when she'd never done it in her life? She came from a privileged home, expected to marry well and raise a family as her mother had done, as she'd been brought up to do. Running away with Roly had brought shame to her family. Stupidly, and very naively, she had thought her parents would come around. That her father, himself a self-made man, would accept Roly, a simple boatman, into the family as a son-in-law. They'd be given a nice house, as her father had given her eldest sister on her marriage. But what she'd failed to realise was her mother's influence. The shame, the scandal had been too much for her mother.

Her family had cut all ties, pretended she didn't exist. Roly had said it didn't matter. That he'd look after her forever. She believed him, of course she did. He was her husband, the one she could rely on. Yet, as the years went by, Roly worked away more and more, leaving her to fend for herself in surroundings she wasn't used to, would never get used to.

Pausing in the shelter of a doorway, Georgiana tried to think what to do next. Frankie would be wanting a feed soon. She'd have to go home, back to the freezing hovel, back to quiet Iris and her questioning fearful eyes. The poor girl hadn't been the same since Roly's funeral. She'd huddled alongside Georgiana in the rain as the coffin was lowered into a pauper's grave. While Georgiana had sobbed for her darling Roly, Iris had remained dry-eyed and frightened.

What went on in her daughter's little head?

'Mind out, missus,' a man uttered, wanting to get through the doorway she cowered in.

'Forgive me.' She stepped out into the falling snow and continued along Goodramgate until she entered one of the narrow snickets of the Bedern slum area. Head down, she slipped past men loitering, smoking in the stairwell, and went up to Dorrie's rooms.

'How did you get on, lass?' Dorrie asked, sitting in front of the fire with Frankie on her lap. She was changing his wet napkin.

'No good.' Georgiana sighed, feeling useless and disillusioned. She sat on a chair by the fire, holding her ice-cold hands out to the warmth. Dorrie's three rooms were filled with the debris of a large family. The two rooms off the main room were the bedrooms for Dorrie's children, while her and Sam's bed was pushed into a corner of the main room. A large table dominated the rest of the space.

'Get a cup of tea down you.' Dorrie placed Frankie over her shoulder and with one hand stirred the pot of stew simmering on the fire. 'You're going to have to start asking for work at the factories. You can read and write, it'll stand you in good stead.'

'The factories are twelve-hour shifts, what am I to do with Frankie for that long? He's only three weeks old. I need to feed him.'

'I can take in Iris, no problem,' Dorrie offered kindly. 'You'll have to find someone to feed Frankie while you're at work.'

She reared back at the thought. 'I don't want another woman feeding him. He's my son.'

'Aye, and what use are you to him if no money is coming in to keep a roof over his head?'

Georgiana sighed and sipped the weak black tea.

'Listen, lass, Freida Shortman, from across the yard, is still feeding her youngest. I'm sure she'll feed Frankie for you while you're at work.'

'She's so filthy, Dorrie, and smells of urine and Lord knows what else. We see her all the time drinking gin from a bottle she keeps in her bodice.'

'What choice do you have, lass?'

'I need a job where I can take Frankie with me.'

'Aye, and the likelihood of that is as much as me becoming Queen of England,' Dorrie huffed. 'Get yourself off to the factories tomorrow morning. If you get taken on, then I'll look after Frankie and only take him to Freida when he's hungry, will that do? I don't know what she'll charge, mind. Knowing Freida, she'll not be cheap.'

Tears welled and Georgiana felt lost for words at the enormity of a bleak future stretching out before, a future where she would have to give her baby to another woman to breastfeed. She reached for Frankie and, undoing her bodice, fed him, which made the tears slip over her lashes and run down her cheeks. How had her life come to this?

'You know, lass,' Dorrie added coal to the fire, 'you could always go to your family and tell them what's happened.'

'I don't believe they would care, Dorrie.' She sniffed, stroking her son's little head.

'But it's different now. You're alone. A widow. They might want to help, especially as you've got the young'uns. It's worth a try. What have you got to lose?'

Georgiana nodded. 'You're right. I have nothing to lose. I'll go tomorrow.'

'Take both children with you, show them what they are missing out on,' Dorrie said craftily. 'The buggers should never have shown you the door just because you loved a man of a lower class.'

'If that doesn't work, I'll go to the factories.' She felt overwhelmed with it all. Falling in love with Roly had cost her so much, only his love in return had compensated her. Without him, she was adrift, lost.

Dorrie poured another cup of tea. 'If nothing else, try and get some money from your father. The rent is due in a few days. I bet you've none left of the cash Roly's boss gave you?'

Weary of the struggle, Georgiana shook her head. 'No. I paid the rent for a month, up to this week. The bit left over I bought food with, but it's all gone.'

'Oh, lass. I can barely feed my own, but you're welcome to eat with us tonight.'

'What would I do without you, Dorrie?' She fought back another bout of tears.

Dorrie patted her hand. 'Let's just hope your family take you in.'

The snow had stopped overnight, but the morning was bitterly cold and grey as Georgiana led Iris along the slippery streets. Snow had drifted into corners of buildings and lay on rooftops. She held Frankie wrapped up in a blanket, his face covered from the biting wind. Dorrie had given Iris an extra shawl to wear on the long walk from Bedern, across the river to the other side of York. Blossom Street was a wealthy part of York, where the rich men of the town lived in spacious houses surrounded by bountiful gardens.

Such a lengthy walk in the icy conditions soon had them flagging in energy. Georgiana wished she'd the money for a hansom or even a seat on the omnibus, but she didn't and so they trudged along, their toes going numb from their wet and cold boots. Iris's cheeks were red, and her steps slowed.

Georgiana, who'd washed her hair last night, knew she looked far from presentable. Her coat was showing signs of wear and her skirt had inches of slush around the hem. The black felt hat she wore was out of shape and she had holes in her gloves.

'Is it much further, Mam?' Iris asked.

'No, just a few houses along.' Heart racing, Georgiana stared at the passing houses, her one-time neighbours who'd she'd not seen for seven years. Mouth dry, she finally stopped at a black wrought-iron gate. Before her, the childhood home she'd adored stood in its imposing grandeur. Large sash windows in a pale sandstone brick gave the house a welcoming feel, but Georgiana wondered if she'd receive the same from the inhabitants inside.

She glanced down at Iris's rosy face, pinched with cold. 'Come on then.'

With a determination she didn't quite believe in, she pushed open the gate and walked up the wide path to the front steps. She'd timed the visit for before nine o'clock to give her the chance to see her father alone and before her mother came downstairs.

She rang the pull bell and waited.

The door opened and a tall man in forest green livery gave her an inquisitive stare. 'May I help you?'

'Yes.' Georgiana took a deep breath. She'd been expecting Turling, the family butler. 'I would like to speak to my father, please.'

'Your father?' The footman frowned, clearly not believing her.

'Mr Shaw.'

'Mr Shaw is not at home, I'm afraid.'

'He will want to know I am here,' she spoke with her old manner, as a daughter of the house, despite her wretched appearance.

'Who is at the door, Thomas?' A female voice came from behind.

Georgiana didn't recognise it and tried to peer over Thomas's shoulder for a better look.

'It's a woman, madam. Asking after the master.'

An older woman came into view, her grey hair up in a neat arrangement on her head, pearls at her throat and she wore a day dress of navy wool and fine lace. Her small eyes narrowed at Georgiana. 'Who are you?'

'I'm Mrs Georgiana Carter. I was Georgiana Shaw.'

The woman's eyes widened for a second before narrowing again on taking in Georgiana's appearance. 'So, *you* say?'

'It is the truth. I would like to speak to my father, please.'

'That is not possible.' The woman dismissed Thomas with a flick of her head. 'Your father has no desire to ever see you again.'

'And who are you, madam?' Georgiana spoke, her annoyance mounting.

'I am his wife!'

The words echoed around her brain. *Wife?* 'That's not possible. What are you saying?'

'I'm saying that your mother died three years ago, and your father has remarried. To me.' The triumphant declaration swelled the woman's bosom. 'I am Mrs Shaw.'

'My mother is dead?' She felt unearthed, as though drifting above the scene on the doorstep. Her mother was dead and buried these three years and she had no idea. How had she not known her own mother was dead?

Of course, she wouldn't have known, she inwardly chided herself. She didn't read the newspapers because she couldn't afford to buy them. None of her family knew where she lived, and she'd not once seen any member of her family in seven years. It wasn't as if they'd enter the slums of Bedern for any reason, just as she'd given up her rights to mix with her family's society and attend balls and the theatre. Their worlds were divided and because of her decision to be with Roly, she'd lost her family. None of it was fair, but then when was life ever fair?

'Now, if you would remove yourself from my doorstep, I would be obliged.' Mrs Shaw muttered with distaste, giving Georgiana a once-over and clearly finding what she saw to her dislike.

'I must speak with my father. It's very urgent. He would want to see me, and his grandchildren.' Georgiana dragged Iris forward. 'Let him tell me to my face that he won't see me.'

'I think not.' Mrs Shaw took a step back to close the door.

'My sister then?' She thought quickly. Perhaps Athena would take them in. 'Tell me where she lives, please.'

'Your sister has moved to Derbyshire to be closer to her husband's family. I very much doubt she will wish to be disturbed by you.'

Deflated, Georgiana held Frankie tighter. 'I just want to see my father.'

'He does not want to see you. You mean nothing to this family. Do not come here again or I shall call the police.' The door snapped shut.

For a moment Georgiana could only stare blindly at the black wood before her. She remembered the last look her mother gave her as she left the house, suitcase in hand. Her mother's lofty expression showed all her disappointment and the tightness of her pursed lips kept back the damning words she clearly wished she could say. They had never been close. Her mother wouldn't allow it, denying love and emotion to her two daughters, but Father had been softer, more inclined to tenderness, a kind word, a pat on the shoulder.

Georgiana longed for a kind word now.

'Mam?' Iris whispered.

Aware of the cold wind, the low grey clouds promising more snow, and the heaviness of Frankie in her arms, she smiled at her little girl with more fortitude than she felt. 'Let's go home.'

As they retraced their steps towards the city centre, Georgianna tried to plan. She needed money desperately. Finding work was necessary to keep them from the workhouse. She had to avoid that at all costs.

The journey across the city took longer as Iris became weary and slow. Frankie started grizzling, nuzzling for the breast. Tired and dispirited, Georgiana was glad to finally make it up to her room.

Iris flopped onto the bed, while Georgiana fed Frankie who fussed and whined.

Dorrie entered, a worried look on her face. 'You're back then. How did it go?'

'My mother has died, and my father has remarried, and his wife told me rather plainly that I am not wanted.'

'Dear God.'

Georgianna blinked back tears. 'There will be no aid from that quarter.'

'And none from Freida either.'

'What do you mean?' She tried to give Frankie the nipple, but he turned his face away.

'Freida's only gone and moved in with another man down Walmgate way.'

'But she has a husband.'

Dorrie sniffed with disgust. 'Aye, and she don't want him anymore. The poor man has been raging all morning fit to kill someone. But she's packed and gone, leaving her six kiddies behind.'

Georgiana buried her face in one hand. 'What am I to do?'

'We'll get by somehow, lass.'

'But how, Dorrie?' She managed to get Frankie to latch on, but his suckling was in fits and starts.

'Try the markets in the morning. Perhaps there's a stallholder who'll let you work a few hours with Frankie strapped to you.' Dorrie scratched under her armpit. 'Or you could do a bit of cleaning at some of the pubs?'

'Yes. I could take Frankie with me, and he could sleep in a box while I cleaned.'

Dorrie nodded enthusiastically. 'That's the spirit. There's work out there if you're willing to find it.'

'I hope you're right.' Frowning, she gazed down at Frankie, noticing his little face was red and hot to touch. 'Dorrie, Frankie is hot and fussy.'

'Let me look at him.' Dorrie took the baby and stripped him from his blanket. Lifting his nightgown, her eyes widened. 'He's a bit red, yes, not a rash as such…'

'A rash?' Georgiana panicked. 'He needs a doctor.'

'Aye and what are you going to pay him?' Dorrie tutted.

A knock on the door brought their heads up.

Dorrie marched over and opened it. 'Yes? Oh, it's you.' She glanced back over her shoulder to Georgiana. 'It's the rent man.'

'I'm paid up until the end of the week,' Georgiana defended, standing up, her heart pounding in her chest.

The man pushed the door open fully and peered in with a disdainful sniff. He waved a piece of paper. 'It's your notice. You're to be out by next week.'

'But why?' She gasped in horror.

'You're a widow with little 'uns. You've no way of earning and paying your rent. You're out, missus. That's all there is to it.' He placed the piece of paper on the floor and walked away.

She felt faint.

'Mam, I'm hungry,' Iris murmured from the bed and was ignored.

'Oh, lass,' Dorrie whispered, her shocked tone matched Georgiana's state of mind.

'What am I to do, Dorrie?'

'I'd take you in, lass, but we're bursting at the seams as it is.'

She crumbled onto the edge of the bed as Frankie began to wail. 'I can't go to the workhouse…'

Chapter Five

Slipping on her gloves, Victoria checked her desk for any letters she might have missed. Satisfied she'd collected them all into her bag, she pinned on her woollen hat. Outside, teeming rain caused the windows to steam and she hated the thought of leaving her warm office to go out into the foul weather, but she had to make the last post and then call on Harriet and possibly Aunt Esther if time allowed. She'd promised to be back in time for the evening meal with the children and read them a story before bedtime.

'There you are.' Mercy breezed into the office only to stop on seeing Victoria was about to leave. 'I didn't know you were going out?'

'The post office. I must send my reply to the *Yorkshire Gazette* about the article they printed regarding the sorry state of the sewers in the poorer areas. I don't why I have to keep defending the people of those areas and how they must live like rats when town councillors keep turning a blind eye to it all. I have petitioned the authorities several times this year and attended the chamber meetings to what end? To be ignored continuously. Well, I've had enough, and my complaints will now be broadcasted in the newspapers. I will take to task any newspaper who refuses to print my letters to the editors.'

'It's a never-ending struggle, I know.' Mercy tilted her head as cries came from the school room. 'Any replies to the advertisement to the teacher's post?'

'None that are suitable.' Victoria walked to the front door.

Mercy followed a few steps behind. 'I've just come from the hospital, Joseph says the Wilkes family who arrived yesterday all have scarlet fever. He's isolating them in the hospital. We need to make sure no one else ventures there.'

'That is a worry.' Victorian frowned. New inmates at the home usually brought with them disease or vermin from the streets. On admittance they were all bathed and deloused at Joseph's cottage hospital and kept there for twenty-four hours as a short quarantine before being allowed to enter the main buildings of the home and mix with the other women and children.

'I'm telling all the mothers now before I spend an hour in the school room. I'm going to teach the children a new song to sing for Christmas.'

Victoria wrapped her cloak about her and opened the door to the icy elements. Her carriage was waiting for her at the bottom of the steps. 'I shan't be too long.'

'Mama?' Ettie, her daughter, came running along the entrance hall. 'Can I come with you?'

'No, sweetness, not today.'

'But I wanted to tell you about the drawing I've done.' Her delicate features crumpled in disappointment. She was a mini version of Victoria with a sweet manner and generous spirit.

'You can show me this evening when I come home,' Victorian soothed her, and then hurried down the steps to the carriage. She glanced back and saw Mercy take Ettie's hand and close the door. 'Post office, Percy, thank you,' she called up to the driver.

In the carriage, she stared out at the passing rain-washed street, the barren fields of winter and the bare trees. The Home she and Joseph had built for women and children was on the

Huntingdon Road on the outskirts of the city, but close enough to be only a short carriage ride away.

Soon the fields gave way to the narrow, cobbled streets. They passed under Monkbar and along Goodramgate where numerous horse-drawn vehicles impeded their progress. Patiently she waited, warm under the thick blanket over her knees. Some of the shop windows had Christmas decorations up and holly wreaths on their doors. Victoria did enjoy Christmas. She glanced at the people hurrying by in the rain, women covering their heads with shawls, baskets full, men ducked into the nearest public house to have a pint of ale while children dangerously darted between carriages and wagons and men pushing wheelbarrows and handcarts.

As her carriage waited to move forward in the traffic, Victoria watched a wet and bedraggled cat slip out of a ginnel between two terraces and jump over a stone wall. A woman leant against the entrance to the ginnel, bent over and pale. Her face full of despair, the baby in her arms crying.

Quickly, Victoria leaned out of the window and told Percy to wait, before climbing down the carriage step and rushing over to the woman. 'Can I help you, madam?'

The woman stared at Victoria as though not really seeing her, the baby wailing in her arms. 'I must get home…'

Instantly, Victoria recognised her tone of voice, a well-spoken woman not of the working class, yet she looked working class. Her threadbare shawl pulled over her head was dirty and had tattered. Her dress was stained, her lank hair unkempt and she was terribly thin with sunken cheeks and shadows beneath her eyes.

'I can assist you,' Victorian said, taking the woman's elbow. 'Would you permit me to hold the baby?'

'No!' The women reared away. 'He's sick.'

'Shall we take him to a doctor then?'

'I can't afford a doctor. I can't afford anything.' A wretched sob broke from the woman, and she bent double as though in pain.

'Are you hurt?'

The woman swayed. 'No…'

Victoria caught her as her knees gave way. 'I've got you. You'll be fine,' she murmured, looking around for help. No one was in the ginnel, the driving rain sending most indoors. Half carrying, half dragging the woman, Victoria got her to a stairwell of a tenement and eased her down onto the bottom of the stairs. Two little girls on the landing above stared down at them.

'Good day.' Victoria smiled up at them. 'Do you know this lady?'

The children ran off calling for someone.

Crouching in front of the woman, Victoria took one of her cold hands. 'I'm going to get help. Stay right here and I'll be straight back.'

'I must get home… He's wet…ill…'

'Do you live far?'

Dazed, the woman didn't answer, and her eyes closed.

Outside the stairwell, the rain came down in a torrent, drowning out any other noise. Leaving the woman, Victoria gathered up her skirts and mounted the stairs to the next floor, intending to knock on doors for help to get the woman back to her carriage.

Coming along the corridor were the two little girls and an older woman, looking worried. 'May I help you, madam?'

Victoria let out a breath. 'Yes, there is a mother and her baby downstairs. They are ill.' She went back down to the sick woman with the others following.

'Ye Gods, Georgiana, what possessed you to go out in this weather?' The older woman leaned over the younger one called Georgiana. 'Why didn't you stay at the hospital until the weather cleared?'

'She says her son is ill,' Victoria said.

'Aye, he's been raked with fever for a week. We can't afford a doctor, but she said she was going to take him to the hospital this morning.' The older woman straightened. 'I'm Dorrie Turner, that's my two girls there, and this is Georgiana Carter.'

'Victoria Ashton.'

Dorrie gave a nod and then looked back down at Georgiana. 'She's not in a good way. Her husband died over a month ago when the baby was born. She can't find work and feed the baby at the same time. She's been evicted so she and her little girl, Iris, have been sleeping in with us, but were squashed like fish in a barrel. I've eight kids of me own still at home, and me old man, now with Georgiana, the baby and Iris we're thirteen.'

'Gracious!' Victoria had seen overcrowding first-hand in her work, and before her marriage to Joseph, when she'd been thrown out of home herself, she had experienced living in the slums with Mercy. 'I run the Ashton Women and Children's Home. I can take Georgiana home with me.'

'She ain't going into no institution!' Dorrie flared up as though Victoria spoke of a prison, which most people thought institutions were, especially the workhouse, and they'd not be far wrong.

'No, please, don't think that my home for women is anything like the workhouse. I assure you it isn't. You can come with me and see for yourself if you like.'

'Aye, I will, for I'm not leaving her anywhere she'll be separated from her children.'

'No, I promise you. We do not do that. My husband is a doctor, and he will take care of all three of them and then, when they are well, they can live in the main house until the time comes when Georgiana feels she can find work.'

'Right, well, I'll hold you to that, Mrs Ashton.' Dorrie started up the stairs. 'I'll fetch Iris and their things.'

It didn't take long for Victoria and Dorrie to have the little family in the carriage and they were heading back to the home. The rain didn't stop, creating large puddles in the roads which bounced them around on the seat.

Victoria sensed Iris was frightened, her little hand held by Dorrie, the older woman looking about with interest as they rumbled through the wide iron gates and down the gravel drive behind the main building.

'We have a cottage hospital, Mrs Turner,' Victoria informed her. 'My husband is a well-respected doctor.'

When the carriage stopped before the stone cottage, the rain eased slightly. Victoria called for Joseph, but it was his nurse, Dahlia, who came running out of the front door, her snowy white apron a flash of brightness in a grey dull day.

'Ah, Dahlia, do help us get Mrs Carter and her children into the hospital.'

Dorrie marched in after them, still holding Iris's hand tightly. She gave the once over to the front office before joining them in the warm, white-painted room where Joseph examined new patients. Although it was a hospital, Victoria didn't want it to look austere and so paintings hung on the wall and a fire glowed in the grate. In summer, flowers in vases adorned the surfaces with the windows open to let in fresh air and bird song.

'Doctor Ashton is just sewing some stitches in young Charlie Porter's hand, the boy cut himself when chopping wood,' Dahlia said, assisting Victoria to lay Georgiana down on the bed.

'What was he doing with an axe?' Victoria took the tiny baby gently and laid him in a cot in the corner.

'He said Agnes needed more wood for the fire in the laundry.' Dahlia slipped off Georgiana's worn and weathered shoes and the loose socks which were wet from the holes in the shoes.

'What are you doing with her things?' Dorrie stepped forward.

'Mrs Carter will be given a warm soothing bath, Mrs Turner, as will the children,' Victoria explained, 'once my husband has examined them. We have new clothes for them to wear.'

'Like prison uniforms?' Dorrie's eyes widened.

'No, not at all. They are new clothes which are donated by people. My good friend, Harriet Drysdale, has a haberdashery in Fossgate. She makes dresses and children's clothes for us.'

'Oh, I know of that shop. I once went in and bought some buttons.' Dorrie relaxed a little. 'She's your friend you say?'

'One of my best. I could not do without Harriet.' Victoria smiled in reassurance.

Joseph entered the room and Victoria quickly made the introductions. Georgiana was half asleep with exhaustion on the bed.

'I'll examine Mrs Carter and then the children,' Joseph said, washing his hands in the basin under the window.

'Iris won't let you touch her,' Dorrie told him. 'I'll have to stay.'

Joseph smiled kindly, drying his hands. 'That is no problem, Mrs Turner. Whatever makes Iris comfortable is fine by me.'

'Shall I make us some tea?' Victoria said.

'Tea?' Dorrie spluttered, eyes wide. 'You make tea?'

'Oh, yes, Mrs Turner. I do many things that I learned while living in Walmgate.'

'You lived in Walmgate?'

'I did, in the worst part of it.' Victoria patted her arm. 'I'll find us some cake, too.'

An hour later, with Georgiana examined, bathed and tucked up in bed sleeping peacefully, Victoria helped Dorrie bath Iris and Frankie in a small room off the kitchen.

'I can't remember when I had a good soak in the bath,' Dorrie said, soaping up Iris who grumbled when she had to have her hair washed. 'I used to go to the public baths, but, well, time and money soon put paid to that as my family grew bigger. Besides, carrying buckets of water upstairs is a never-ending job. We don't have enough for cooking never mind washing.'

'I remember that all too well,' Victoria said, washing Frankie's tiny body, and noticing the napkin rash on his buttocks from staying in wet napkins for too long.

'I find it hard to believe you lived in the slums, Mrs Ashton. Not a lady like you,' Dorrie said, shaking her head in amazement.

'I fell on hard times, just as Georgiana has done.'

Iris splashed and gave a small chuckle as the water sloshed over the side of the bath.

Victoria grinned. 'All children enjoy a good bath. My son, Matthew, is five and the mess he makes at bath time you wouldn't believe.' She laughed gently. 'My daughters refuse to go anywhere near him in fear of getting wet through.'

'From what I've seen here, you run a good establishment, Mrs Ashton.'

'We try to, Mrs Turner, and I feel we succeed most of the time. There are some women who refuse our help and sneak out in the night and back to the dangerous lanes of the slums.'

'Georgiana won't. I can assure you of that.' Dorrie lifted Iris out of the bath and started drying her. 'This little family needs some help. I've done me best, but I can't look after them properly. I don't have the money or the room. I've me own family to think of and a sick son of my own.'

'Naturally, Mrs Turner,' Victoria agreed. 'But *we* are here now. Mrs Carter will receive all our assistance to regain some sense of normality again. My husband told me that all three are malnourished. Frankie has signs of a fever.'

'She's had a tough time. Even before her husband died, Georgiana found it difficult to adjust to life amongst us.'

'Oh?' Intrigued, she lifted Frankie out of the basin and dried him in front of the fire.

'Aye, Georgiana is from a good family, decently brought up. The other day, she went to her father's house on Blossom Street to ask for help but got sent packing. Mr Shaw has remarried, and the new wife wants nothing to do with them.'

'Shaw?' Victoria wrapped Frankie in a warm blanket and held him over her shoulder as he started to cry. 'I know of the Shaw family.'

'You do?' Dorrie was impressed. 'Then you might be able to speak to them?'

'I'll certainly try, but Mrs Shaw is rather bigoted about our good works. I've only met her a few times at fundraising events, and she had much to say about all sorts of things.' Victoria dressed Frankie, remembering the second Mrs Shaw as an over-bearing woman who was too opinionated on subjects such as saving the women of the streets. Mrs Shaw felt those women were not worth time nor money. Victoria had stern words with her, and they'd not spoken since.

'I'd best be getting back, my Sam will think I've done a runner.' Dorrie slipped a cotton shift over Iris's thin body and then over that a woollen dress of dark brown that Mercy had found for her. 'You can put your socks on, lass, can't you?'

'Where's my mam?' Iris asked, her bottom lip trembling.

'I shall take you and Frankie to her.' Victoria took her hand. 'Your mother is sleeping, but you can lie beside her if you want?'

They went back into the room where Georgiana lay in bed, but who woke on hearing Frankie crying.

'I think he needs a feed.' Victoria handed him over to Georgiana. 'I'll let you say your goodbye to Dorrie, and I'll arrange for a meal tray for you all.' As Victoria turned to go, Mrs Turner held out her hand.

'Thank you, Mrs Ashton, you and your husband. It's a load off my mind that Georgiana and the little 'uns are going to be looked after. May I come and visit again?'

'Absolutely, Mrs Turner. You are welcome any time, and if you know of any women needing our help, please don't hesitate to let me know or tell them about our home. I'll have the carriage take you home. H, and my husband will come and examine you son, if you wish?'

Dorrie's expression fell. 'I've no money for doctor's bills, I'm afraid.'

'There will be no charge, Mrs Turner. I'll speak to my husband.'

In the corridor, Victoria nearly bumped into Joseph.

He took her hands. 'Everything all right?'

'Yes, I was just going to fetch a meal for them.'

'I've already seen to it. I asked Mrs Shelton for chicken broth and bread and butter. It will be a good start. Nothing rich. They must eat slowly for their stomachs are so shrunken they will be sick if they eat too fast or too much.'

'No pudding then?' She smiled, linking her arm through his as they walked to his office.

'Tomorrow they can have pudding.' He paused, worry creasing his brow. 'You saved them just in time, my love. Another day and I think the situation could have been vastly different. The baby is not getting enough milk, the mother is starving herself to give what food she has to her daughter.'

'I'm so pleased I saw her by chance through the carriage window.' She paced the small office. 'I think it is time I started doing the rounds of the slums again. I've been so busy with the administration side of things recently that I've forgotten that there are women out there who don't know about us and who need help.'

'You're busy because we get enough women coming to the front gates begging for help. We are full to bursting at all times, there is no need to go looking for the destitute when they walk up the drive so frequently.'

'It shouldn't mean I turn my back on others out there.'

He placed his hands on her shoulders. 'I know I can't stop you, nor do I want to, but I ask you to be careful. Work is hard to come by in winter when the farmers aren't hiring. People become desperate. Do not go alone, I beg you.'

'I won't. I'll take Mercy.' She kissed him and walked to the door. 'Oh, by the way, Georgiana was a Shaw. The Shaws from Blossom Street. They were neighbours down the street from my uncle's house. I know them, or at least Aunt Esther knew the first Mrs Shaw quite well. She attended her funeral. Mr Shaw has remarried, as you might know, and I've met the second Mrs Shaw a few times at charity events.'

'And?' Joseph looked at her from over a medical journal he'd opened.

'Georgiana was turned away at the door by her step-mother. I doubt her father even knows of her current situation.'

'Darling.' Joseph raised his eyebrows at her. 'Don't get involved.'

'How can I possibly not?'

He sighed, knowing her too well.

'And can you visit Mrs Turner's son. He's ill.

'Has she left yet?'

'No, not yet. I said I'll have the carriage take her home.

'Then I shall return with her and see him.' He closed his book.

'Thank you, my darling.' She left the office, her mind set on speaking with Mr Shaw as soon as she could, and then she remembered she'd forgotten to post her letters!

Chapter Six

Ruthie woke to crashing in the other room. She eased up on her elbow, wincing at the aches in her body. The events of the last two days came flooding back. On Sunday night Gerald had been out with his mates and brought them back to their rooms. All night they had drunk and laughed, played cards and fought with one another. She'd stayed in her room, petrified that one of them might come in. The door had no lock and when the handle turned and someone sneaked in, she'd screamed fit to wake the dead.

Thankfully, the fellow had returned to the main room to a chorus of jeers. Ruthie had pushed her bed hard against the door in case anyone else wanted to try their luck.

Then yesterday, she'd woken early, intending to walk the icy streets to work before Gerald and his mates woke, but on leaving her bedroom, the foul stench of vomit and urine made her stomach churn. Her vomit had joined the other mess on the floor, waking the men up. With curses and yawns, the men took themselves off to work while Gerald eyed her from his bed.

'Why were you sick?'

'The smell in here is disgusting,' she groaned, her stomach heaving again.

He shot out of bed, wearing the same clothes he'd worn all week. He stank and needed a shave. His sour breath wafted over her as he peered down at her. 'You were off colour the other day, too, when you were cooking onions.'

Ruthie shrank inside herself, ducking her head. 'Is it any wonder living in this dump?'

Gerald gripped her upper arms, bruising her skin. 'You're lying.'

'Let me go. I've to get to work!'

He shook her like a rag doll. 'I didn't believe the rumours that you were keen on that Irish Mick upstairs, but maybe they were true.'

'No, don't be stupid,' she lied.

'Stupid? You're calling me stupid, are you?' His hand slapped her hard across the face.

She cried out, cupping her left cheek. 'Don't, Gerald. I've got to get to work.'

'Are you friends with that Irish scum?'

'No!' she defended, knowing to tell him the truth would be the end of both her and Micky when he returned.

He flung her away. 'You're not going to work.'

'What?' Shocked, she stared at him. 'I have to!'

'Not anymore. You're not working for the Coledales' again. I'll tell them this afternoon. You're to stay here and clean up this place.' He grabbed his coat from the hook at the back of the door.

'We need the money,' she pleaded. 'It's a good job, Gerald.'

'I'll get you another job. Once close by. There's a few shifts going at The Crown.'

'I'm not working in a pub.' The idea horrified her.

He advanced on her again, fist raised. 'You'll bloody work where I say you will. I'm not letting you out of my sight and when that Irish Paddy comes back, we'll be having words.'

'There's no need, Gerald.'

His gaze dropped to her stomach. 'Time will tell if you're lying to me.'

All day she'd been in a state, alternating between crying and raging as she cleaned up sick and spilt ale, emptied piss pots and scrubbed the room. The one spark of happiness had been finding five shillings under the table that one of the fellows had dropped. She'd slipped that into the pocket she'd sewed in her shift.

That night, Gerald had come home, irritable and hungover. He'd bought a bag of coal and a small crate of vegetables along with a scrag end of some beef cut and a bottle of beer.

In silence, she'd cooked a stew, while he crowed with delight at telling her he'd got her wages due from the Coledales'. However, he gave her none of it.

Later, after they'd eaten, she tentatively asked for some money, and he'd smacked her in the head and then punched her in the back as she turned away from him. He'd stormed off to the pub, but not before terrorising her in the room for ten minutes.

Now, as another day dawned and the noise from people above and in the stairwell heralded another exodus of those who had work, Ruthie gingerly climbed out of her bed. Her bare feet touched the freezing wooden boards.

She listened for any sound in the other room. Had Gerald left for work?

A sudden banging on her bedroom door made her jump. She stifled a scream with her hands.

'Ruthie! Get up, you lazy baggage! I'm off to work, but you've got a shift at The Crown at three. Don't be late and show me up. I'll call in after work.'

Her mouth dry, she continued to stare at the door.

'Ruthie! Do you hear me?'

'Ye-yes…'

'Three o'clock at The Crown.'

'Yes.' She waited to hear the other door open and shut and then slowly pushed her bed away from the door. Shivering with cold, she wrapped her shawl about her shoulders and went into the main room. The fire had gone out. Gratefully, she didn't feel sick this morning and took advantage of the cold potatoes left over from dinner the night before.

Taking the empty buckets, she left the room to fill them up from the pump in the yard. The snow-filled wind took her breath away and cut through her clothes to chill her. A line snaked from the tenement to the pump with women and children waiting to fill buckets.

Shivering, Ruthie stood in line, her shawl over her head to protect her from the worst of the icy wind. She spotted Niamh O'Dowd coming along the line carrying two full buckets. 'Niamh.'

'Hey there, Ruthie.'

'Any word on Micky?' She didn't speak loudly, not wanting the neighbours to hear.

Niamh paused. 'We got a letter on Friday. Mammy's coming back, but Micky's staying on. He's managed to get a fine position as an assistant steward at the big house, would you believe?' Niamh boasted with pride.

'The big house?' She couldn't believe he'd got himself a job. He had to come back to York, to her.

Niamh put down the buckets and folded her arms as though ready for a good natter. 'Aye, on our landlord's estate. Micky's new position will mean the old folk won't be driven out. Micky can pay their rent and look after them, so he can.'

'But he had a job here. Can't they all come here?' A shiver of dread ran over her skin.

'Nay, the old folk won't leave Ireland. It broke their heart that we left, but Micky has returned to them and their happy enough with that, so they are. We always knew our Micky was better than the rest of us. He can read and write, don't you know? He sounded happy in his letter.'

'Did he mention me at all?' The line moved forward but Ruthie stayed where she was. This was more important than getting water.

'You? Why would he mention you, pray?'

'We… We are friends.' The fear of Mickey never returning to her made her feel clammy and ice-cold at the same time.

Niamh laughed. 'Micky is friends with everyone.'

'But he *will* come back?' Ruthie forced herself to sound hopeful when she was dying inside.

'Not likely, Ruthie. To be sure he's not going to give up a good position to come back here and work as a labourer on the railways. One day he might be steward himself with his own cottage, imagine that? No, Ireland is where Micky needs to be for the sake of the family.'

Ruthie shuddered with foreboding. 'Perhaps I can write to him?'

Niamh's eyes narrowed with sudden hostility. 'Why would *you* want to write to him?'

'Well, he… he and me… we…'

'Listen, Ruthie, our Micky is making something of himself. There's nothing in this filthy place worth coming back for.'

'I could go to him then?'

'You go to him? He's never once mentioned you.' Niamh gave her a cutting look. 'So why would *you* go to my brother? Do you think there's some kind of understanding between you both? Has our Mickey promised you anything?'

'Yes… well…'

'Tell me!' Niamh demanded.

'Micky has to come back…' Ruthie reddened in embarrassment. 'Because I'm in the family way, Niamh. Micky has to marry me.'

Niamh gripped Ruthie's arm tightly, bruising her flesh. 'Are you saying my brother is responsible, you little tart?' she sneered, all friendliness gone.

Ruthie nodded, close to tears. 'It's the truth. He said he loved me.'

'Loved *you* and you *believed* him? Well, more fool you,' she mocked. 'Decent girls wait for a ring on their finger before they lift their skirts for a man.' Niamh's nails dug into Ruthie's arm. 'You tell anyone that kid is Micky's and I'll do for you, understand? He's not wasting his life on a silly cow like you. Micky's forgotten all about you and you'd best forget about him. He's never coming back.' Niamh picked up her buckets and stormed off.

Shaking, Ruthie stepped to the back of the line and wiped away the tear that fell. It couldn't be true. Micky said he loved her. She believed him. He said she was his girl. *His girl.* He couldn't lie about that. He had loved her, she knew it. He'd kissed her so passionately, so tenderly, always whispering in her ear how much he adored her. She didn't know a lot about love, but she couldn't have imagined his kisses meant nothing? He couldn't fake that, surely? Micky enjoyed being with her and she let him have her body to show him how much she loved him.

She groaned in despair, making the young lad in front of her turn around and stare at her.

She filled her buckets without thought and dragged them back up the stairs. She made the fire and boiled the kettle. She needed to wash but it seemed beyond her. All she could do was sit and hold her tea as it went cold in her hands.

Without Micky, she was ruined. Tears flowed freely, trickling off her chin to soak the front of her dress. Without Micky she was destined to a life of disgrace and gossip. How was she to cope as an unmarried mother? Gerald would kill her, of that she was certain.

Her desperation grew with each passing hour. Ruthie couldn't think or move. The church bells tolled the time as the day crawled by slowly. She'd have to go away. It was the only answer. Gerald would murder her if he found out she was with child and the O'Dowds' weren't going to help her. What did she have left?

She was too numb to cry, too shocked to make a serious plan. Why did this have to happen to her? Why did she fall for Micky O'Dowd's lies and smooth talking?

Abruptly, the door banged open with such force it broke one of the hinges. Gerald stood, his face red with rage, puffing like a bull about to charge.

Ruthie blinked at him. 'What is it?'

With a roar, Gerald lunged for her, picking her up by the neck, squeezing until she thought she'd pass out. She couldn't breathe. Her lungs and mind screamed silently for air. She tried to kick him, push him away but he was too strong. He was going to kill her.

Suddenly, he flung her from him onto the floor and bent over her. 'You stupid bloody idiot! I could kill you! Kill you with my bare hands!'

In a flash, her fear turned to anger. 'Do it then!' she screamed back, tired of fighting him, tired of worrying about upsetting him, tired of fearing him. 'I want to die. Do you hear me? I want to *die*. So, *kill* me, go on! *Do it!*'

Gerald stepped back at her shrieking, her furious face. 'You were meant to be at The Crown an hour ago.'

She'd forgotten. Her shift at the pub had completely slipped her mind. Wearily, she slumped against the wall. Defeated. Exhausted. Beaten.

'Well?' Gerald kicked at her legs.

Ruthie looked up at him, not even having the energy to hate him. She felt nothing. 'Just leave me alone, Gerald,' she murmured on a deep sigh.

For once he didn't reply or raise his fist. Cursing, he grabbed his hat that had fallen off and marched from the room, slamming the broken door behind him.

Ruthie cried, sobbed, her heartbreak and despair needing an outlet in tears. Eventually, she crawled into bed, but sleep wouldn't come. Her thoughts troubled her too much. She couldn't stay here. Her stomach would soon be growing, and Gerald would demand answers, or even throw her out. To survive she had to make her own decisions. Her fingers touched the five shillings in her secret pocket sewn in her shift. They wouldn't last her long.

The next morning, she waited for Gerald to leave for work before she went into the other room. Ignoring the queasiness she felt, she searched the room for any other money, but there weren't many places to hide money and anyway, she knew Gerald would keep it on him.

The chilliness in the air made her breath visible as she washed her face in the cold water and tidied her hair into a plait before curling it under her old felt hat. She tucked her spare dress and petticoat in a net bag she used for shopping. With a last look about the windowless, dank room, she realised with a pang of regret that she had nothing of her own but the clothes she stood in. Over the years all her parents' belongings had been pawned to feed and house them. Well, Gerald would have to fend for himself now. No longer was she going to be on the receiving end of his fists and boots.

Her plan was to stop by at the Coledales' house and ask for a reference from the housekeeper. A reference would help her gain a new position somewhere, at least for a little while until she was too big to hide her stomach. With her reference in hand, she would walk to the train station and see how far she could get on a few shillings. A new town where no one knew her seemed the perfect solution.

On the landing, she sucked in a breath at the coldness. A door opened on the floor above and then Niamh was coming down the stairs.

'Niamh.' Ruthie put a hand out to her. 'I'm sorry if I upset you.'

'You didn't upset me.' Niamh gave her a smug look. 'I'm not the one who's a fallen little tart no better than a woman off the street corner.'

'I'm not. It's only ever been Micky.'

'Likely story. If you're easy with one, then you're easy with them all. How much do you charge? I bet your brother's friends pay you well.'

'No, I don't do that with anyone. Micky is the only one, I promise you.'

Niamh looked her up and down. 'You're not showing yet.'

'Not yet.'

'Good. Go down to Mrs Cleary in Peel Street. She'll get rid of it for you. It's not cheap mind.'

Ruthie stood still, the words sinking into her brain. Could she get rid of it? It would solve her problem. Was it as easy as that? One visit to Mrs Cleary and she would be sorted? 'I've only got five shillings.'

'Mrs Cleary will take whatever you can give her, I'm sure.' Niamh carried on down the next staircase but stopped at the bottom and looked back at Ruthie. 'Just get rid of it. No good will come of having it, so it won't. Micky won't be marrying you and the family won't help you. Do you want to spend the rest of your life in disgrace, an unwed mother?' She walked out of the building just as a young man entered the stairwell.

Ruthie blushed, hoping the young man hadn't heard Niamh's words. She knew the fellow lived in the cramped attics above. She nodded to him as he passed and gripped the banister, which was a little wobbly, just like her legs.

No baby meant she could get work somewhere decent, maybe a live-in position out in the country far away from here. Gerald would never find out.

She shivered, standing on the freezing landing. She had two choices. Either leave York and keep the baby while somehow finding work and taking care of a child or visit Mrs Cleary and get rid of it before it ruined her life completely.

Step by step she edged her way downstairs, her thoughts whirling in scattered confusion. What should she do?

Outside, snow fell gently, coating the ugliness of the yard in pristine white. Head down, feet dragging, she told herself she was doing the right thing. A quick visit to Mrs Cleary and she'd be free to begin again somewhere nicer than Hurst's Yard.

A short walk led her to Peel Street, but she didn't know which house belonged to Mrs Cleary. A woman, bent over and carrying a basket of food, trod past Ruthie as she stood dithering. 'Excuse me, do you know which house is Mrs Cleary's?'

The older woman stopped, her grey hair covered in a black shawl. ‘I’m Mrs Cleary.’ Ancient eyes gave Ruthie the once over. ‘Follow me.’

Chapter Seven

Coughing into her handkerchief, Victoria waited a moment to catch her breath and then entered the day room. Her weak chest usually caused her some discomfort in winter and spending the last few days out in the cold weather scouring the slums for women who may need help hadn't helped to ease the tightness in her chest.

'Good morning, Mrs Ashton,' one young mother said, pouring out cups of tea.

'Good morning, Susan.' Victoria nodded and smiled to her and the other young woman standing next to her who was cutting slices of cake for the midmorning tea.

Many of the women were seated, knitting or darning before the fire, while children could be heard singing in the classroom next door. In the corner of the room several cots held sleeping babies.

Victoria found Mrs Piper in the corner on her knees picking up toys and putting them into the boxes. Surrounding her were several infants in various stages of crawling or just walking. 'Mrs Piper, may I have a word?'

'Of course, Mrs Ashton.' Mrs Piper stood, a worried look on her young face. 'Is something wrong?'

'No, not at all. In fact, I have received a letter from Digby and Sons.'

‘You have?’ Mrs Piper, a gentle young woman abandoned by her husband six months ago, had come knocking at the front door begging for help. The sick child she held in her arms was close to death and despite Joseph’s diligence and hard work to keep it alive, the little girl had died two days later.

‘Mr Digby has agreed to take you on for a three-month trial at his funeral business in Selby. You’ll be a coffin dresser foremost but also to help prepare the bodies and so forth.’ Victoria wondered if this was such a good position for a mother who’d recently lost her child. ‘You can refuse the offer, and no one will think wrongly of you. I will keep applying on your behalf to other establishments.’

‘It’s fine, Mrs Ashton. I grew up in a funeral shop as I told you when you asked me what skills I have. My mam showed me how to attend to a body before I was ten years old. My grandfather’s funeral business passed down to me father, but when he died and my mother not long after, well I got married to Seth and that was that…’

‘So, I shall write back to Mr Digby and tell him you agree to the offer of employment? He says for you to go to Selby on Sunday evening in order start work on Monday and there’s a room in his loft for you to sleep and his wife has made it comfortable for you.’

‘Aye, it sounds just the ticket, Mrs Ashton, and thank you. I’ve never been to Selby, but I like the thought of a new start in a different place, and it’s not too far away is it.’

‘About fifteen miles, I think.’ Victoria patted Susan’s hand. ‘I’m extremely pleased for you.’

‘It’s all down to you, Mrs Ashton. You try so hard to find us suitable work, you’re a blessing, that’s what you are.’

‘I’ll make the arrangements. Percy will drive you in the carriage after church on Sunday.’ Victoria left the room and headed for her office to answer Mr Digby’s letter.

‘Victoria!’ Harriet came through the front door, bringing in with her a blast of snow-filled air.

'I wasn't expecting you today.' Victoria gave her dear friend a kiss on the cheek and helped her off with her coat.

'Yes, I know but I thought to bring the bundle of blankets I promised you. I gave them to Mercy as I came in. She's outside putting them in the carriage. You're heading out soon?'

'Yes, to Walmgate.'

'I won't hold you up then, but I also came to tell you that Mr DeLacey, you know my friend on Hall Field Road, he has the farm? Well, I was more friends with his late wife, anyway he was the older gentleman looking for help in the house last winter and we sent him Maureen Kelly. Do you remember?'

'Oh, yes?' Victoria led her into her office.

'He has kindly offered us a pig for Christmas. A whole pig. Imagine.' Harriet sat on the sofa before the fire and peeled off her gloves.

'That's very generous.' Victoria added a scoop of coal onto the blaze.

'Indeed. He's extremely grateful for sending Maureen to him. Maureen and her two sons have changed his world, apparently. Maureen sees to the farmhouse and her boys help him on the farm. In repayment he's giving us a pig for Christmas as a way of saying thank you.'

'How wonderful.'

'He's delivering it on the twenty-third, I believe he said. I thought we could have it on a spit on Christmas Eve?' Harriet relaxed against the cushions, she looked tired with shadows under her eyes.

Victoria studied her. 'Are you getting enough sleep?'

'Oh, you know me. I'm a bit of an owl. I like staying up late to get my book work done.'

'You have Jane to help you.'

'Jane is excellent in the shop, but the bookwork is another thing altogether.' Harriet pursed her lips as though in thought. 'That said, I've been pondering on the future.'

'You have?' Victoria sat opposite, intrigued as to why Harriet was considering the future. 'You're not ill, are you?'

'No, a bit tired, but at my age it is to be expected.'

'You're hardly old.'

'I'm sixty-one next birthday, old enough. Which is why I've been thinking. Having no children of my own, I must consider the business when I become too old to manage. I might speak to Mercy and see if she is happy for me to hand it all over to Jane.'

'I don't see why Mercy would mind, it's an honour to Jane. It gives her a secure future in having her own business.'

'That's what I thought, but what of the other children? What do I do about Bobby, Emily and Seth? And your three?' Harriet frowned. 'Yours and Mercy's children are all my godchildren and I love them all. They are my family. I must treat them equally.'

'I doubt Bobby or Seth, or my Matthew would want your haberdashery shop, Harriet,' Victoria joked, then coughed a little.

Harriet grinned. 'Indeed, they wouldn't.'

'Perhaps leave each of them a monetary value in your will?'

'Yes, it's the most sensible solution. I'll visit my solicitor in the new year.'

'Shall I ring for tea?' Victoria stood to pull the bell pull next to the fireplace.

'No, I shan't stop. I suspect you have much to do.'

'I was going to Walmgate. So, I can offer you a lift in the carriage?'

'Lovely. I'll dismiss the hired hansom outside.'

When Harriet returned from paying off the hansom, she entered the office with Kathleen and Ettie. 'These two scallywags were sliding down the banister!' she laughed. 'I caught them!'

Victoria gave her daughters a stern look. 'Not very ladylike, I must say.'

'Sorry, Mama.' Kathleen grinned, clearly not sorry at all. She was tall for her age, all legs and arms, but an emerging beauty was starting to show. 'Papa wanted to speak with you.'

'Papa is here himself,' Joseph said coming into the room. He twitched Kathleen's plait gently. 'I asked you to fetch your mama twenty minutes ago,' he chastised, before giving a kiss of welcome to Harriet.

'Is it important?' Victoria asked him.

'Georgiana Carter and her children. She is well enough to be moved into a dorm. I met Mercy crossing the garden, and she is going to see to it.'

'I'm about to take Harriet home and then go to Walmgate,' Victoria said, placing the fireguard around the fireplace. 'I'll check on Georgiana when I return. Mercy will see her comfortable.'

'I'd rather you didn't go out in this weather,' Joseph said, concern in his eyes. 'You were coughing a lot last night.'

'I feel better this morning and I'll wrap up well.' Victorian cuddled Ettie to her side, her youngest daughter enjoyed embraces much more than Kathleen did. Kathleen believed herself to be too old at nine to be hugged like a baby by her mother.

'If you leave it until tomorrow, I can come with you,' Joseph said, 'but Mary Green is in labour and she's very frightened.'

'Which one is that?' Harriet asked.

'The sixteen-year-old who Joseph found without shoes or a coat on the road into town, remember?'

'Oh yes.' Harriet shook her head sadly. 'Her father had thrown her out when he found out she was with child.'

'Yes.' Joseph nodded. 'It's been many months of getting her to feel safe amongst us. She barely speaks and only settles when I am near. I don't want to leave her.'

'I'm worried she relies on you too much,' Victoria said. Mary, and her dependence on Joseph, had been a subject of much discussion between them. She felt the girl was half in love with Joseph, and her reliance on him would not benefit her when the time came to create a new life outside of the home.

'I shall go with Victoria, Joseph.' Harriet eyed the two of them. 'After a couple of hours, I'll put her in the carriage myself and send her home.' Harriet nodded wisely.

'Thank you, Harriet.' Joseph kissed Victoria's cheek. 'Stay safe. Come, girls, you can help me in the hospital. There are many sheets to fold, and you can keep Mary company.'

Dutifully, the girls followed their father out of the office.

Harriet pulled on her gloves. 'Which part of Walmgate?'

'Last week, Mercy and I visited the tenements from the Foss Bridge up to George Street. So, beyond there is where I'll start today.'

'Did you have much luck helping anyone?'

Victoria sighed. 'A few women listened to me, allowed me to give them money, or bottles of milk for their children, bread… Some are used to seeing me after ten years of walking the lanes, but so many still shun me, see me as not one of them.'

'You aren't one of them. Even when you were living amongst the poor you still were different, from a wealthy background.'

'But they know of me, of what I represent with the home. I'm there for them. Someone they can turn to in times of need.'

'Victoria, you know how they are. Yes, they've seen you walking the streets, giving out aid and charity, but that doesn't mean it's you they'll turn to first. These people are used to being self-reliant. Many might see this home as some kind of workhouse.' Harriet knew how hard it was to get the proud women of the slums to accept help.

'Yes, I understand that, of course I do. Mrs Turner, who is a friend of Georgiana's, our newest guest, even she didn't know what we were. Mrs Turner was frightened that we were a workhouse. I must try harder in getting the message out there about what we do.'

'Word of mouth is the greatest way to advertise.'

'Agreed, but last week we met so many Irish families who didn't speak a word of English. Some came over during the famine thirty years ago and refuse to speak English. The language is a barrier, but they simply do not trust anyone outside of their family, and especially not someone who is English.'

'We do what we can. Isn't that what we always say?' Harriet gave a small smile of encouragement as they donned their coats. 'It's not as if we are empty, is it? The home is always full.'

Outside, Percy had the carriage waiting. Victoria checked the medical supplies, the blankets Harriet brought, and the food baskets made up by the kitchen staff. Satisfied it was all in order, she told Percy her plans and climbed in with Harriet.

The snow drifted down, coating the landscape, obliterating edges of the road until they got closer to the city streets and the snow turned to slush from the numerous horses, carriages and people walking on it. Smoke from thousands of chimneys curled into the dove-grey sky.

They turned into Fossgate and passed Harriet's haberdashery shop, where Jane was rearranging the window display and adding Christmas wreaths and shiny bells. She waved to them as they went by.

'It's such a joy to be able to leave the shop in Jane's capable hands,' Harriet said. 'I have so much more freedom now, and with her living with me gives me company at night.'

'Mercy was telling me this morning that Bobby is thinking of joining the army,' Victoria told her, still surprised by the revelation.

'The army? Interesting. He could have a long career in the army.'

'And be sent somewhere for years on end.' She'd always had a soft spot for Bobby and hated to think of him being sent away with the army.

'Lucky him if he does get sent to somewhere warmer than here,' Harriet chuckled, wrapping her scarf about her chin.

The carriage stopped at the corner of George Street. Victoria, with Harriet's assistance, began knocking on doors of the tenements in St Margaret's Court. The freezing, cold and wet courts and yards were miserable places covered in inches thick mud and refuse. Broken sewer drains seeped onto the cobbles mixing with the strewn rubbish no one bothered to clean up.

Women with blank stares and grubby hands quickly took what Victoria and Harriet held out to them, not answering their questions before slamming doors in their faces. Unperturbed, they carried on, smiling, offering aid, mentioning the home and Joseph's medical care.

'We ain't for the workhouse,' said one ragged-looking woman, a baby in her arms and a small child hanging off her skirts.

'The Ashton Home for Women and Children is a privately governed concern,' Victoria replied. 'We are not a state workhouse or involved with the government in anyway. The home is for women needing a safe place to stay, somewhere they can receive help to better their lives.'

'Better themselves?' The woman swiped at the child pulling at her skirts, but he still clung on. 'I've got a husband, missus, for what good he is. He'd not like me running away to you.'

'No, of course not.' Victoria smiled gently. 'We offer assistance to those women who have nowhere left to go, or who need to escape a dangerous situation.'

'If me 'usband's given me a thrashing it's probably cos I deserved it.'

'No one deserves to be beaten,' she said gently.

'Thanks for the food basket, but I don't need your help.' The woman shut the door in her face.

Sighing, Victoria walked back to the carriage. There were only a few baskets left and a couple of blankets. Cold seeped under her thick warm coat, and her cheeks were chilly.

'Hurst's Yard is next.' Harriet refilled her basket with iodine and bandages. 'I just spoke with a woman who says there's an old woman in a room on the ground floor, opposite the pump, apparently she is ill.'

'We might be able to help her.' Victoria led the way into Hurst's Yard, stepping to one side as a man came along the cobbles with a horse. The air was filled with the ringing of a hammer on iron from the blacksmiths at the bottom of the yard.

'This door?' Victoria asked Harriet, stopping in front of a badly painted door.

'Could be.'

Victoria knocked several times but heard no response. She gently turned the handle and the door opened to reveal a damp and dim room. No fire glowed and the cold musty air made Victoria shiver and cough. On a single bed in the corner an old woman lay smothered in blankets and old coats. Her face was as white as the hair on her head.

'Who are you?' came the croak from the bed.

Relieved the woman wasn't dead, Victoria smiled. 'Good day to you. I'm Victoria and this is Harriet. We were told you've not been well and came to help you.'

'Just let me die.' The old woman lifted a bent and arthritic hand towards the door.

'We cannot do that. What is your name?'

'Aggie… Aggie Littlewood.'

Victoria bent to the fire and raked the ashes. 'We'll not leave until you're warm and fed, Aggie. I'll have my husband come and visit you. He is a doctor.'

'I've no money for a doctor.' The old woman peered at them.

'He won't charge you.'

'That'll be a first then,' Aggie muttered.

Harriet stepped forward, holding a basket of food. 'There's some warm soup here. You'd fancy a sip or two of it, I'm sure.'

'I'll not say no.'

While Harriet eased Aggie up on the bed, Victoria added paper and pieces of wood to start the fire. A bucket of coal was beside the fireplace. Someone was leaving these things here for the old woman.

Victoria soon had a cheery blaze going and the warmth and light it gave brightened Aggie enough for her to sit up and sip the soup Harriet poured into a cup.

'Do you live alone, Aggie?' Victoria asked, banking the fire with coal.

'Aye. Have done for forty years.' Colour had returned to Aggie's cheeks.

'Who brings you the coal?' Victoria asked in a conversational tone while Harriet took the pisspot out to tip into the drain.

'My son did for a bit, but he's gone now. To Canada. Me daughter died two years ago so there's no one left.'

'Do your neighbours call in?' Victoria emptied the basket of food onto the small table in the middle of the room, including a cake of soap and a candle and matches.

'Sometimes. Jim next door does mostly. He fills the water bucket for me and this week he's kept the fire going.' Aggie wheezed as though she'd talked too much.

'If it's becoming difficult for you to live alone, I could find you a place in one of the women's alm-houses.'

'No, I'll not go. I'll die in me own bed,' Aggie said, eyeing Harriet as she came back inside with the empty pot.

Victoria poured out a cup of water for her. 'Very well. I'll come, or someone I trust, will come and visit you twice a week and make sure you have everything you need.'

'Why?' Aggie scowled at her. 'I don't know you.'

'But you soon will.' Victoria grinned. 'Is there anything you need before we go?'

'Only some peace!' Aggie muttered, laying back down on the bed.

Harriet made sure the blankets were tucked up about her chin. 'I'll visit you tomorrow.'

'Do what you like,' Aggie grumbled, but her tone wasn't too harsh.

Out in the yard, the snow fell harder, obliterating the street.

'We should call it a day,' Harriet said, squinting against the snowflakes landing on her lashes.

Before Victoria could reply, a scream echoed out of the nearest tenement. She glanced up at the tall building, checking the windows but there was no movement. The scream came again followed by a roar.

'No, Victoria,' Harriet warned as Victoria took a step towards the stairwell. 'It's time to go. We aren't getting involved.'

'But it sounds as if there's murder being done.'

'Then we'll stop by at the police station and inform them. Let's go.' Harriet dragged at her arm.

Another scream was abruptly cut off.

'Someone is in trouble, Harriet.' Victoria raced for the stairs.

Chapter Eight

Cowering on the bed, Ruthie peered through one eye, the other was swollen shut from Gerald's punch. Every part of her ached, not just ached but throbbed in an agony she'd never experienced before.

Gerald kicked at the wall, his boot going through the damp plaster. 'I can't believe it!' He glared at her, his face ugly with rage. 'Me own sister. A tart! A filthy little slag!'

'I'm sorry…' Blood seeped from the split lip he'd given her.

'Sorry! Sorry? How in hell is that going to fix anything? Me mates are laughing behind me back. Everyone knows that me sister opened her legs for an Irish paddy. A filthy disgusting paddy.' He dragged her from the bed, ignoring the bloodstains on the blankets and her skirts. He punched her in the stomach and flung her to the floor.

Ruthie lay gasping, crying, curling into a ball. She'd been in such horrendous pain since her gruesome visit to Mrs Cleary. She'd been heavily bleeding all night, writhing in agony and this morning she'd been hot with fever, shaking and shivering and the bleeding wouldn't stop.

'Best of all,' Gerald yelled, bending over her, his spittle spraying her face, 'best of all is that you've gone to some skanky old woman to get rid of the paddy's kid like some common street *whore*!'

She groaned, wishing, *praying* she'd die. The agony in her body was unrelenting. Wave after wave of pain washed over her with no let up.

'I'm ashamed of you. You're no sister of mine.' He kicked her in the thigh, ignoring her screams. 'Get out! You're not staying here. You're not decent.'

Suddenly, the door flung open. Ruthie tried to focus on who was shouting, but the pain wracked her body, distorting her senses. Blurred figures came in and out of view.

'Who the bloody hell are you?' Gerald yelled.

Ruthie eased up onto her elbow, peering at the figures in the room. Two women were squaring up to Gerald and he was shouting and cursing, mad with fury.

A woman bent down next to Ruthie. 'You'll be all right. We'll help you.'

Ruthie nodded. The woman was beautiful and smelled so nice, fresh and clean with a hint of flowers. She concentrated on the woman's lovely face while behind her Gerald ranted and raved, smashing what little furniture they had.

Gently, the woman lifted her up and wrapped one arm around Ruthie's waist. 'I'm Mrs Ashton.'

Suddenly, Ruthie stared at her in horror as Gerald quickly advanced on them, yelling fit to burst. He dragged Ruthie from Mrs Ashton's hold and flung her away like a doll. She landed heavy on her side, the pain nearly making her pass out.

In one swift movement, Gerald grabbed Mrs Ashton by the hair and hauled her towards the door. 'I'm not having bloody strangers in my house!'

'No! Gerald! No!' Ruthie scrambled to her feet and lunged for Gerald just as another woman came back into the room, screaming at Gerald. He shook Mrs Ashton by the head, whose face had gone pale with fear and pain.

Ruthie screamed. The world had gone mad. Her brother was the devil.

The older woman hit Gerald over the head with a frying pan, knocking him to the floor. Frantic, the woman pulled Mrs

Ashton to her, holding her tightly. 'Victoria, dearest. Where are you hurt?'

'It's nothing, Harriet.' Mrs Ashton winced, her shaking fingers pulling out her hatpins which hardly held her hat in place anymore. Her copper-coloured hair fell about her face in a messy abundance.

'We're leaving now,' the woman named Harriet ordered.

Mrs Ashton turned to Ruthie. 'Come with us, please?'

Needing no second bidding, Ruthie limped towards the two women and they both held her upright between them.

'Is there anything you wish to take?' Mrs Ashton asked at the door.

Feverish, Ruthie turned to look back at the wrecked room and her unconscious brother on the floor. 'Nothing at all.'

The three of them hobbled down to the yard. Some of the neighbours peeked out of their windows but Ruthie didn't care. She was never coming back here, not ever. Let them talk and gossip, she was done.

It seemed right when Mrs Ashton and Harriet climbed into a shiny carriage. It confirmed to Ruthie that they were important. They helped her up onto the seat and arranged a blanket over her, but she couldn't stop shivering. She clenched her teeth at the pain in her stomach and groin.

'We're taking you to my home,' Mrs Ashton said, trying to tidy her hair. She was rather pale, and her hands continued to shake as she fussed with strands of her hair.

'Let me do it, Victoria.' Harriet pulled her hands down. 'Joseph will go mad when he sees you.'

'We *don't* mention it to Joseph,' Mrs Ashton snapped. 'Promise me, Harriet. I'll tell him later, tomorrow.'

'As soon as he looks at you, he'll know something happened.'

'He'll be busy with Mary and her labour. I just need a cup of tea.'

'And a brandy,' Harriet added, her manner sharp.

'What your name?' Mrs Ashton asked Ruthie.

'Ruthie Benson,' she answered, voice faint with pain as the carriage wheels rumbled over the cobbles jolting her body.

'We'll take care of you, Ruthie. This is my friend, Harriet Drysdale.'

'Was that your husband?' Harriet asked.

Ruthie closed her eyes, feeling sick. 'My brother.'

'Do you have any other family?' Mrs Ashton asked.

'No. I have no family.' Ruthie felt utterly alone and wretched.

As they turned in through the high iron gates, Ruthie peered with one eye out of the window at the grand building and gardens.

'This is the Ashton Home for Women and Children,' Mrs Ashton told her. 'You'll be safe here.'

Harriet opened the door as the carriage stopped. She helped Mrs Ashton down first and then they both assisted Ruthie. She felt more blood flow from her, and her legs gave way.

'Run for help, Harriet,' Mrs Ashton instructed, taking Ruthie's weight. 'You're bleeding heavily, Ruthie.'

'I paid… for someone to get rid… of my baby,' she murmured, clinging for dear life to Mrs Ashton. She was dying.

'I see. Well, soon you'll be comfortable, and my husband will tend to you.'

Another woman came rushing down the stairs and took Ruthie's other arm.

'We'll need Joseph, Mercy,' Mrs Aston said.

'Harriet is already going to the hospital.' Mercy gave Mrs Ashton a queer look. 'She's in a right state. What about you? Oh lord, Victoria, what happened to you?'

'I'm fine.' Mrs Ashton took a deep breath as they made it up the short steps and inside where she firmly closed the large door.

Ruthie barely noted the grand entrance with yellow walls and cared little about it. She just wanted to lie down and die as quickly as possible. Somehow, she made it along the corridors without collapsing. Mrs Ashton and Mercy settled her onto a bed and warm blankets were placed over her.

Mercy held a cup to her lips, encouraging her to drink the foul-tasting liquid. 'It'll help with the pain, Ruthie,' she told her. 'I'm Mercy Felling. I'll be looking after you.' Her kind face was the last thing Ruthie remembered.

Waking up, Ruthie felt disoriented. A lamp was lit beside the bed, a fire blazed in the grate from what she could see out of one eye. She moved one hand and her body ached in protest at the slightest movement.

'There now, you're all right,' a whisper came.

Turning her head, Ruthie tried to remember the woman's face.

'I'm Mercy. Mrs Ashton's friend.'

'Mercy,' Ruthie said on a sigh as events came crashing back into her mind.

'You've been asleep for four hours. It's late.' Mercy gave her some water to sip.

'Where am I?' Ruthie could only remember a tall ceiling and yellow painted walls.

Mercy placed the glass on the side table. 'The Ashton Home for Women and Children. We will take care of you.'

'It's not a workhouse?' The thought scared Ruthie.

'Not at all. I promise you. We are a home that gives medical aid and shelter for women who are homeless or abandoned, their children, too. You are free to leave whenever you want, but we hope you'll stay until you are well again.'

'My brother won't find me?' She pictured Gerald, his fist raised ready to smash her in the face.

'No, and after what he's done, he'll likely be staying at Her Majesty's pleasure for some time.' Mercy straightened the sheets.

'Prison?' She couldn't believe it. Gerald would be crazy mad now.

'Hopefully. Victoria, I mean Mrs Ashton, her husband, Doctor Ashton and Harriet have all given statements about what he's done to you. Your brother has been arrested.'

'Good.' Ruthie relaxed against the pillows, wincing at the little stabs of pain that darted around her body. 'Is Mrs Ashton all right? Mr brother wasn't gentle with her.'

Mercy gave a small smile of reassurance. 'Victoria is stronger than she looks, believe me. It'll take more than that to knock her down. She's been on the receiving end of rough hands many times before in the last ten years. Unfortunately, we both have. It's part of the world we venture into. We aren't always welcome.'

'I'm glad you came to my rescue. I think Gerald would have killed me otherwise.'

Mercy held her hand. 'The woman you went to…'

Ruthie blushed with shame. 'Mrs Cleary.'

'Yes. She has done some damage to you, inside. Joseph, Doctor Ashton, had to stitch you. You're going to be terribly sore for some time.'

'I thought something was wrong. It hurt so bad, and I couldn't stop bleeding.'

'The woman should be in jail, too. Doctor Ashton will compile a complaint against her, but she can easily deny everything. It's your word against hers, unless we can find more women to speak against her.'

'I doubt that will happen.' Ruthie sighed. 'There's too many women who have more than enough children and women like Mrs Cleary helps to get rid of another mouth to feed. No one will speak against her in a court.'

'Sadly, you are correct.' Mercy leaned forward, an earnest look in her eyes. 'We want you to stay with us until you're healed and then we can see what we can do about setting you up in a new life. How does that sound?'

'It sounds too good to be true. Why are you helping me?'

'Because that's what we do.' Mercy smiled proudly. 'Mrs Ashton built this home to give aid to those less fortunate. She once suffered being homeless herself and knows how it feels to be without comfort, family, hope.' Mercy straightened, her tone brightening. 'Now, are you hungry?'

'No, not really.' She felt too sore to move.

'Supper will be in an hour. Tea and toast with jam and a slice of fruit cake. Perhaps you might fancy that when it comes?'

Ruthie took a deep breath. Tea and toast with jam and a slice of fruit cake. Ruthie's chest swelled with emotion. She'd not eaten anything decent for weeks, not since her last meal when she worked at the Coledales'.

'Rest now. Doctor Ashton will come in soon and examine you again.' Mercy sat back on the chair by the bed. 'Would you like me to read to you?'

'Read to me?' Ruthie stared at her. No one had ever read a story to her in her life.

'Yes, I was going to begin a new book. Thomas Hardy's *The Trumpet Major*. Shall we see if it's any good?' Mercy's smile was such a nice sight when usually all Ruthie received was snarls and beatings. The worry of being with child and trauma of getting rid of it, the rejection of Micky, and Niamh's and Gerald's hatred dimmed a little.

'I'd like that.' A tear rolled down Ruthie's cheek at this woman's compassion, at all their kindness. Her body ached, but she would do her best to ignore it. Instead, she'd listen to Mercy's lovely voice and lose herself in the story.

Chapter Nine

'I'm asking you not to go, please?' Joseph's expression tightened.

Victoria walked to the other side of the desk. Beyond the office, the sounds of the children playing in the schoolroom ebbed and flowed. 'I feel I owe it to Mrs Carter to speak to her father. Mr Shaw should be aware of his daughter's predicament. Georgiana will need assistance to get past her stepmother's barricades.'

'I understand that but send a letter instead.' Joseph leaned his hands on the desk. 'The snow is thick out there and your cough remains. You've been assaulted by a thug and refuse to rest.'

'It's not the first time I've been in such a situation, Joseph, and unlikely to be the last,' she said dismissively.

'Which is my point. I do not want you out there in dangerous weather conditions when you've been though such an ordeal. Heavens, Victoria, you are still badly shaken. You had a nightmare last night. You must rest, I beg you.'

'I will, later.' The nightmare she'd experienced last night left her frightened. She'd been thrown into a cellar and left to die by someone whose face she couldn't see. She'd cried out for Joseph, drenched in sweat.

Joseph glared at her. 'We both know that's a lie.'

‘There’s much to do…’ As tired as she felt, she wouldn’t allow the incident with Gerald Benson to stop her plans for Christmas.

‘And there are enough of us to do it, without you making yourself ill.’

‘Joseph, don’t fuss, please?’ Her head pounded.

‘Fuss? God forbid I fuss over my wife! Tomorrow is Christmas Eve, everyone is excited about the party, the pig on the spit, the opening of presents. My parents are coming this afternoon if the trains can make it through the snow. How will you feel if you are ill in bed and can’t enjoy it? And what about Christmas Day? It’s the one day we, your family, are to have you all to ourselves.’ He ran his hands through his dark hair, which was beginning to be sprinkled with grey. ‘You promised me this Christmas it would be just us. I share you with fifty other women and all their children throughout the year, and I’m happy to do that. However, you promised that this Christmas we’d be together, alone, our family, Mercy and the children and Harriet, my parents. That’s it. Us, together. No strangers demanding your time. I want you to be well to enjoy it!’

‘All right!’ Victoria held up her hands in surrender.

He shrugged. ‘Forgive me if I sound selfish, but is it too much to ask to have one day with my wife without interference?’

She softened her stance and went to him. Laying her head on his shoulder, she relaxed as his arms came around her. ‘I won’t go to Blossom Street to see Mr Shaw or Aunt Esther. You are right, the snow is too thick, and I don’t want to become ill and spend Christmas in bed. Aunt Esther is probably visiting Stella, anyway.’

His arms tightened at the mention of her cousin Stella, an evil woman who in the past made Victoria’s life very difficult. Stella’s vile accusations about Victoria causing the death of her father, Victoria’s uncle, still lingered. The family had believed Stella and thrown Victoria out of the house. Stella had also tried to turn Joseph away from Victoria, for Stella wanted him for herself.

All that had happened in the past shaped Victoria into who she was now, but although Aunt Esther had made amends, Victoria had nothing to do with two of her cousins, Stella or her awful brother, Laurence. The only cousin she liked was Todd and he was rarely back in York.

'Send a letter to Mr Shaw and please stay inside where it's warm.' Joseph kissed her. 'Tonight, we shall have mulled wine and fruit pies and listen to the children sing carols. You know how much they enjoy that.'

She nodded and stepped out of his arms as the door opened and Mercy walked in carrying the mail.

'Ruthie is running a bit of a fever, Joseph,' Mercy said.

'I'll go and examine her, but it's not surprising after Mrs Cleary's dangerous efforts.'

'Oh, and there's a telegram just delivered.' She gave it to Joseph who read it.

'Mother and Father can't make it to York.' He looked sadly at Victoria. 'Their train was halted at Doncaster. Snow is stopping trains heading to Leeds. They've returned to Lincoln.'

'How unfortunate. The children will be so disappointed,' Victoria said, standing close to him to read the telegram. 'Matthew was wanting to show his grandpapa his progress on the piano and Kathleen wanted your mother to see her embroidery sample. Ettie thought to dance for them.'

'We shall take the children for a visit to Lincoln once the snow thaws.' Joseph tucked the telegram into his waistcoat pocket. 'We've not been to my parents' house in a year. It's time we took the children more often now they are older.'

'Yes, I agree. It's important for them to spend time with their grandparents and your extended family. We shall all write to them tonight and hopefully the mail will get through.'

When Joseph had left the room, Victoria sat behind the desk to write a letter to Mr Shaw.

'We have so many season salutations from previous women we've helped begin new lives.' Mercy sorted through the mail, reading one postcard and letter after another. 'I've been putting the postcards on the mantlepiece in the sitting room, to show our current guests that those before them have prospered.'

'An excellent idea.' Victoria read the ones Mercy gave to her.

'However, I do think Sally Gold may wish to leave against our advice.' Mercy opened the last envelope.

'Why?'

'Someone came to the gates yesterday evening, a man, probably her husband.' Mercy's tone was resigned. 'Now she's saying that its time she went home.'

'Her husband kicked her out and took up with another.' Victoria played with her pen. 'What is stopping him from doing it again?'

'Nothing, of course. Sally believes he has changed. His fancy-piece has left, apparently.' Mercy placed the cards in a neat pile. 'Sally has already packed her things.'

'Very well. If she's made her decision.' Victoria knew that trying to persuade some of the women to stay could be futile at times, especially when they missed home, or the man they ran from begs them to return. So many women feel ashamed to be living away from their homes, their husbands, no matter how bad those men can be.

'I've asked Mrs Shelton to make up a food basket for her. Percy will take her into town in an hour if he can get through.'

Victoria glanced out of the large window, white blanketed the gardens and the fields beyond. 'Give Sally my best wishes.'

Mercy reached over and patted Victoria's hand. 'Sally was never going to be the one who would stay and start her life over again. For the five weeks she's been here, she's never stopped talking about her husband. For all his faults, she loves him, and she's wanted to go home all the time.'

'Then good luck to her. I hope her husband mends his ways.' Even as she said the words, she knew it was highly unlikely. How many times in the last ten years had they repeatedly taken in the same woman because her husband never stopped the beatings, the gambling, the emotional abuse, the neglect?

It was heart-breaking to mend some of these women only for them to come seeking aid months later. They never turned them away, but each time they arrived, they would say it was their fault and, once healthy again, they'd return to the same situation. The cycle, for some, was never broken. Victoria had long accepted it, even if it pained her. Instead, she had to focus on the good stories, those women who left behind the abuse, or who had been abandoned, and who went on to create new lives with meaning and happiness.

'Harriet said she was closing the shop early and she and Jane will be here before one o'clock.' Mercy gathered the cards and stood. 'I've made up Harriet's bed in my cottage as she is staying with us to save her going back and forth into town, especially in this weather.'

'Good idea. I'll be finished soon and join you with our mothers. I can hear the children are becoming excited.' She cocked her ear, listening to the sounds of boisterous children.

Mercy laughed. 'Yes, some of the mothers are becoming harassed. I shall endeavour to read them a story to calm them, but I doubt I'll be successful.'

After finishing her letter, Victoria hurried over to the stables, careful not to slip on the snowy path Mr Nevis and Robbie had been clearing all morning.

The frigid air caught at her chest, and she coughed for several moments. Her lungs protested at the iciness, but she continued and reached the stables. A small fire was lit in the tack room where young Fred, the stable groom, oiled a leather harness. In the main carriage barn, Percy polished the carriage. 'Ah, Percy.' She paused to cough again.

'Nay, madam, you shouldn't be out in this with your chest.' His expression was one of concern. Percy had been her driver ever since they built the home and was a gentle soul, but who protected Victoria like a personal guard whenever they went out in the carriage to visit the slums.

'I'll only be a minute. Can you take young Fred with you when you drive Sally Gold home? I want him to deliver a letter to the Shaw's residence on Blossom Street.'

'We'll be lucky to get through, madam,' Percy said, wiping down the carriage door. 'It depends if the streets have been cleared across town.'

'Indeed, and if you cannot make it to Blossom Street, I fully understand. I can post the letter another day, but I would like Mr Shaw to receive it today, if possible.'

'Right you are, madam.' Percy nodded, taking the letter from her.

She paused before leaving the barn. 'Is young Fred staying here for the celebrations or going home to his family?'

'He's going home, madam, with your permission. His father is very poorly, and young Fred is mighty worried about him.'

'Then I'll ask Mrs Shelton to make up a food basket for Fred to take home with him. Drop him off on your way back, Percy, so he can be with his family. We have no need of him for a few days, do we?'

'No, madam. I doubt you or Doctor Ashton will be wanting the carriage for a day or two?'

'No, we won't be.' Victoria smiled. 'My husband has forbidden any of us from leaving the grounds in this weather.'

'A sensible plan.'

'It will give you a break, too. Don't stay in your room the whole time, come to kitchen where it's warm and Mrs Shelton can feed you.'

'Thank you, Mrs Ashton. I do enjoy a cup of tea in the warm kitchen chatting with Mrs Shelton and the maids.'

'With that said, I'd best get back inside before my husband finds out I'm not by the fire.'

'You're fully recovered from the ordeal in Hurst's Yard, madam?' he asked with a worried frown.

'Absolutely, Percy. Thank you for coming to our aid and getting us home quickly.' She smiled and with a nod went back across the gardens.

Despite her words, she still shivered whenever she thought of Gerald Benson dragging her across the room by her hair. Physical assault was never easy to overcome, but she had in the past when her visits to the slums had brought her into contact with men who were bullies and evil cowards who delighted in frightening women and those of a lesser size than themselves.

No matter how terrified she became, she would always stand up to those people who used violence to get their own way. It gave Joseph great concern, but he knew she'd not behave any other way. She'd never turn her back on someone needing help, even when she herself was in danger.

Chapter Ten

Christmas Eve dawned clear and bright. The bright light shining from a winter's sun streamed through the gaps in the curtains at the tall dormitory windows, blinding the women and children awake.

Georgiana sat up in the double bed, one of five in this room. Iris slept soundly and between them Frankie was stirring. As the other mothers sleepily whispered to their children to stay quiet, or to use the potty, Georgiana put Frankie to the breast and let him feed.

It amazed her how in the space of a couple of weeks, Iris had seemed to grow, and Frankie looked like a chubby, normal healthy baby. She herself had added flesh under her skin. Her bones no longer protruded from near starvation. Her hair, once lank and riddled with lice had been washed several times, deloused and cut to a manageable length just below her shoulders, and which she could twist and secure with combs she'd been given.

Their clothes, mere filthy rags, she, Iris and Frankie arrived in, had been burnt and replaced with clean smelling items of good quality. She'd smiled when Iris had beamed at the lovely navy woollen dress given to her, complete with a white pinafore and black boots. Frankie wore embroidered little gowns and was wrapped in a white blanket to keep him warm.

For herself, for once Georgiana didn't feel ashamed. Her unkempt state of dress and dirtiness had been replaced with smart clothes and cleanliness. The threadbare garments she once continually darned and patched which denoted her low status in life were gone. Instead, she now wore a black skirt and bodice, thick petticoats, a clean corset and cotton chemise. Woollen stocking and black boots added to her sense of renewal. To be respectfully fitted out in mourning clothes for dear Roly gave her strength to face the future.

She and Iris had nightgowns, something she'd not owned for years, not since the one she packed from home when she first married Roly had fallen into pieces from too much use.

The difference was not only in body but in mind. With the old money worries lifted off her shoulders, Georgiana could think positively about the weeks ahead. Yes, she missed Roly, but their marriage had been one of struggle, of his frequent long absences, the uncertainty of having enough money to pay the rent and feed themselves. With all that gone, she felt lighter, able to hold her head up again.

She could see a future ahead, especially with Mrs Ashton and Mercy's generous help. There was a chance she could have rooms of her own one day in town, a job of some sort when Frankie was old enough to be left with someone. She didn't know how it was all to come about but Mrs Ashton had spoken to her a few days ago and told her not to worry. Georgiana and the children could stay at the home for as long as needed. The relief was immense, and she vowed to do all that she could to turn her life around, to succeed in never returning to live in the slums of Bedern again.

The bell rang for breakfast, and Georgiana woke Iris and told her to get dressed while she changed Frankie's napkin.

On a normal day, two young nannies, employed by the home, took the babies and ushered the small children under five into the nursery on the attic floor, giving the mothers time to eat their breakfast downstairs and spend the morning sorting out washing to deposit in the laundry and then joining the others for lessons in various rooms downstairs.

Many of the poorer women had become mothers at a young age, usually straight out of school. Many were illiterate and there were lessons in reading and writing given by the nearby church warden. There were also cooking lessons given by Mrs Shelton, housekeeping lessons given by Mercy, sewing and haberdashery lessons run by Harriet Drysdale. When the weather was fine the women could go out into the vast gardens and learn how to grow vegetables from Mr Nevis and Robbie.

But today was different. Christmas Eve. A holiday for all.

For the first time in a long time, Georgiana wanted to smile, be cheerful. True, she had nothing, owned nothing but the clothes she wore, but at least she and her children were warm and fed. Iris played happily with the other children staying at the home and was coming out of her shell more each day as Georgiana grew stronger in health and peace of mind.

After giving Frankie to one of the nannies, Georgiana took Iris's hand and went downstairs to the dining hall. She grabbed two plates at the buffet table and helped herself to eggs and bacon, toast and tea and a smaller portion for Iris. She sat at the long tables with the other women and the older children who ate with the adults. She was beginning to know one or two mothers. Some were happy to chat, while some remained aloof, or were shy and not wanting to make friends.

'Good morning, everyone.' Mercy stood in the doorway, smiling happily. 'Merry Christmas Eve to all. This morning after breakfast we, the staff here, thought we'd have some parlour games with you all, including the older children until our midday meal. After that, this afternoon, we'll have presents to open for everyone. Then some carol singing before supper. Snow has fallen heavily again overnight but the sun is shining this morning so far, therefore if any children wish to go outside and play, perhaps build a snowman, that would be a nice way for them to let off some steam.'

As Mercy walked around the dining hall speaking to the women, Georgiana ate her breakfast, not needing to encourage Iris to eat, for although her daughter still ate in her dainty way, she was consuming more of the wholesome food each day. Iris missed Dorrie and the Turner family, but Georgiana was determined that her daughter wouldn't suffer the depravity of the slums ever again. They would visit Dorrie, of course, but Georgiana was keen to move on away from the reminders of the past.

'Ah, Mrs Carter.' Mrs Ashton was suddenly beside her.

Georgiana looked up, her fork halfway to her mouth with the last of her bacon. 'Yes, Mrs Ashton?'

'When you have finished your breakfast, would you come to my office please?'

'Of course.' Georgiana swallowed. 'Am I in trouble?'

'Oh no, not at all.' Mrs Ashton smiled and patted her shoulder, then smiled at Iris. 'You look very pretty today, Iris,' she said before walking away.

'What have you done then?' The woman opposite Georgiana grinned cheekily, adding sugar to her teacup. 'I bet they want to give you a job here.'

'Really?' Georgiana frowned at the woman who she believed was called Dolly.

'Aye, course they do. You can read and write, can't you and you talk posh.'

'I can read and write, yes.'

Dolly nodded wisely, before wiping the nose of her small son sitting beside her. 'Mrs Ashton is looking for a helper in her office, apparently. I overheard Mercy and Doctor Ashton talking about it yesterday. They want Mrs Ashton to take it a bit easy, see, so she can rest more with that cough of hers.'

'Oh, I see.' The news gave her pause for thought. A job here at the home? Did she want to live here permanently? She wasn't sure. In her mind she wanted a place of her own. Somewhere close to fields for Iris and Frankie to run about and play in. Was she aiming too high? This home was preferable to a dank poky attic room in some tenement.

Dolly, who had a nasty scar running from her chin down her neck and under her bodice, reportedly from a knife attack, sipped her tea. 'I'll look after your lass, if you want? Take her in to play some of the games.'

'Thank you.' Georgiana explained to Iris that she'd be back shortly and to stay with Dolly and her son.

Then, somewhat nervous, Georgiana crossed the wide entrance hall, past the empty schoolroom and to the front of the building to Mrs Ashton's office near the entrance.

She checked her clothes were neat, her hair tidy in the black ribbon she'd used to bind it up, then knocked and waited. When bid to enter, she walked in with her back straight.

Her surprise on seeing her father standing near the fireplace next to Mrs Ashton stole her breath away.

Mrs Ashton hurried to her side and took her arm. 'Please, Georgiana, come and sit down. Your father is here to see you.'

For a long moment Georgiana stood and stared at the man who'd turned his back on her. The one man she always thought she could rely on, but who the minute she did something he didn't agree with, denounced her as his daughter and closed his heart to her.

'Will you not come and sit down?' Mrs Ashton asked in her kind voice.

Allowing to be led to the sofa in front of the gentle warmth of the fire, Georgiana sat down gratefully, for her knees were shaking. 'Why are you here? How did you find me?'

Her father rocked slightly on his heels, hands behind his back, neck stiff and his eyes didn't meet hers. He looked older, fatter. The pale grey hair sparse on his head. Yet he still was a handsome man, in control and sure of himself.

Mrs Ashton sat beside her. 'I wrote to him, Georgiana. I hope you don't mind. However, since you told me that you had failed to be allowed through the front door of your former home, I took matters into my own hands and decided a letter to your father was in order.'

She stared up at her father, emotions whirling through her. In his presence she was a girl again, a girl wanting to impress him and failing, always failing. 'I'm surprised you came. I thought I was dead to you. Isn't that what you told me the day you told me to leave the house?'

'I have not come to rake over old wounds, Georgiana.' His chest expanded on a deep breath. 'Mrs Ashton wrote to me of your circumstances. Your husband is dead.'

She winced at the mention of Roly. 'He is.'

'But you look well.'

'That is due only to the kindness and generosity of Mrs Ashton. I was close to death when she found me. The children wouldn't have lasted much longer either.'

'Children?' His chin lifted and a light entered his eyes. He turned to Mrs Ashton. 'You didn't inform me of grandchildren.'

'That is for Georgiana to tell,' Mrs Ashton replied.

Georgiana stared at him, realising that she was stronger now than when she left his house. He didn't frighten her. She didn't need his approval. 'Yes. You have a granddaughter and a baby grandson.'

He blinked as though absorbing the news he was a grandfather.

'I take it my sister has also given you grandchildren?'

'Your sister no longer speaks to me. She has moved away with her husband. As far as I know they have no children.'

'Why doesn't she speak to you?'

His cheeks flushed red. 'I believe she is displeased that I remarried. She and my wife do not get on.'

'The same woman who refused me entry when I was needing you and sick with ill health and desperation? That woman?'

He swallowed and pulled at his collar. 'My wife can be… difficult.'

'I didn't even know of Mama's death,' she said accusingly. 'You robbed me of that.'

'You did that to yourself when you chose that *boatman* over your family!' he retorted, his fists balled by his side.

Mrs Ashton stood and rang the bell pull. 'I believe that talking of the past will not be beneficial to either of you. I shall order some tea, and I suggest that the conversation should be of the future. Do you not agree, Mr Shaw?' Head tilted, her tone gave no room for argument.

The order for tea was given to a maid and then Mrs Ashton resumed her seat and waved Georgiana's father to the wing-backed chair on the other side of the fireplace. 'Now, Mr Shaw, I do trust you have not ventured out to this side of York through the snow on Christmas Eve to simply argue with your daughter?'

'Indeed, I did not,' he huffed.

'Then I suggest that you begin discussing with Georgiana the ideas you put to me when you first arrived?'

'What ideas?' Georgiana asked, gazing from one to the other. 'I am not a child to be talked about without consultation.'

'Undeniably, and please do not think any discussion we had was to your disadvantage,' Mrs Ashton told her gently.

'We want what is best for you,' her father said.

'How do you know what is best for me? You've had nothing to do with me or my family for seven years.' She glared at him, angry at his lack of love and support for all those years when she desperately needed her father. 'My life could have been very different if you hadn't rejected me on my marriage. I have suffered like you couldn't imagine, me and the children have lived worse than animals!'

'Georgiana, please.' He put his hand up to stop her words.

'Please what, Father? Please don't tell you the truth of what you've put me through?'

'You had a husband to provide for you,' he snapped. 'You wouldn't listen to me when I told you he was not worthy, and you paid the price. How is any of that my fault?'

'Because you could have helped me,' Georgiana whispered, emotion choking her. 'I needed my father, and he wasn't there.'

Mrs Ashton held her hand. 'You are not alone. You have us and your father is here now.'

'Georgiana…' Her father sighed heavily, unhappily, his grey eyebrows drawn together. 'I do not want us to be separate any longer. It has been difficult for me since your mother died. There have been many changes in my life… I'm growing older…' His look was one of sorrow. 'I would sincerely enjoy having you home again. I would like to get to know my grandchildren.'

Georgiana's heart thudded. 'Do you mean that?'

'Of course, I do,' he huffed, offended that she should doubt him.

A maid brought in the tea tray and Mrs Ashton poured out the tea, which no one touched.

She looked at Mrs Ashton. 'May the children come in?'

'Absolutely.' Mrs Ashton left the room to fetch them.

'Iris, my daughter, looks the image of Mother,' Georgiana warned him.

'She does?' He seemed surprised by that.

The door opened and Mrs Ashton entered carrying a sleeping Frankie, while Iris shyly hurried over to sit next Georgiana.

'Don't be frightened, poppet.' Georgiana smiled. 'This man is my father, your grandfather.'

Mrs Ashton boldly placed Frankie into his startled grandfather's arms. 'There, Mr Shaw, meet your grandson, and isn't your granddaughter such a pretty little thing?'

'Indeed…' He gazed from Iris to the baby in his arms. 'I've not held a baby since you were tiny, Georgiana,' he said in wonder.

Tears clogged her throat at the sight of her burly father holding her baby son. She never thought she'd see such a day as this. '*They* are your legacy, Father.'

He nodded, eyes watery, overcome with emotion. He cleared his throat slightly. 'You must come home, daughter. I will look after you and the children.'

She sighed in great relief. At last, she was to have some of her family in her life again, but the picture of her stepmother's scorn rose up to cloud her happiness. 'I would like that, too, Father, but what of your wife? She made it clear she doesn't want us.'

He rubbed his chin in thought. 'It will be challenging, I won't deny it.' He stared down at Frankie's sweet rosy face. 'Perhaps it might be best for me to buy you a house of your own, somewhere close, where I can visit?'

She blinked in surprise. A house of her own? Dare she hope? Dare she imagine such a thing could be true?

Her father smiled at Iris. 'She is your mother's image, and you named her after her favourite flower.'

'I'm glad you remembered.' Georgiana allowed the tears to fall. 'When I had nothing, the only thing that gave me comfort was the memories of what my life used to be like, when I was a child and happy. When Mother indulged us with lessons in the conservatory of her favourite plants, of walks in the garden when she'd point out different flowers to us. I adored those times with Mother because normally she had little to do with Athena and me. She was always so busy with other things.'

'The garden was your mother's preferred place to be.'

Mrs Ashton rose. 'I shall leave you alone to talk.'

Georgiana passed the plate of tarts to Iris for her to take one before replacing it on the tea tray. 'Father, I would like to stay here until you do buy a house for us. Iris is settled here, and I do not wish to return home to live with a woman who doesn't want us. It may take some time for you to sort out a home for us.'

'Stay here? In a home?' He bristled. 'I do not want my daughter and grandchildren staying in a Women's Home.'

'Why? It is far better than where I have been living, I can assure you.'

'Everything is different now.'

'Is it?' She couldn't hide her fears.

'Are you doubting me?'

'Forgive me, but trusting you isn't something that will come easily to me. You threw me out once before and said awful, unkind things to me. So, yes, I will not easily believe everything you say. I must take care of my children and right at this moment, staying here is the best thing for us all.'

His cheeks reddened. 'What I did in the past is unforgiveable. But the error of my ways has been shown to me several times. I lost you, then my wife, then I remarried in haste because I didn't want to be alone.' He sighed. 'Athena married and moved away because of her stepmother. We barely see her. She never forgave me for sending you away.'

Georgiana's chest swelled with love for her sister. She missed Athena terribly. 'Will you give me Athena's address, please? I would like to write to her.'

'She would consider that a blessing. I believed she tried to find you a few years ago, but we did not know your married name. I thought it was Robins or Roberts.'

'If you had listened to me when I first told you about Roly, things might have been very different, but you only heard the words boatman and nothing more.'

He nodded. 'As I say, my past decisions have given me much grief. It's time to put things right.' He stood and gave Frankie to Georgiana before bending down to Iris. 'I will call again tomorrow, little one, with presents.' He glanced at Georgiana. 'That is if you wish me to?'

'Yes, Father, I would like that, but it will be Christmas Day, what will your wife say to that?'

'My wife will not have a say. She kept from me that you'd come to the house. I wouldn't have known about your situation if Mrs Ashton hadn't written to me. My wife will not keep me from my girls anymore. I shall return home and begin making plans about buying you a house.' He paused. 'I will never let you down again, Georgiana.'

Impulsively, Georgiana stood and leaned forward to kiss her father's whiskery cheek. 'Thank you, Father.'

He smiled and straightened his shoulders. 'Until tomorrow then.'

She watched him leave the room and found suddenly that her legs were shaking so much she had to sit down. Iris placed her hand in hers. Georgiana gave her a teary smile. 'We're going to be fine now, sweetheart, just fine.'

Chapter Eleven

Ruthie woke from a nap to the sound of children squealing. At first, she was disoriented. Then, realising she was in a room in the hospital, she relaxed. Earlier she'd been hot with fever, shivering and clammy. Her body ached with every movement. Doctor Ashton had given her some medicine and another examination. He'd sat with her for a long time until she felt asleep and remembered no more.

Now, she felt calmer, and not so ill. She was sore, but the pain had receded somewhat. The dull ache was easier to handle than the sharp pains. One eye remained swollen shut, but her lip had stopped bleeding and the griping pains down below had eased.

The clock on the mantle above the glowing fire showed it to be afternoon, and children's voices could be heard outside the window. They sounded so happy. Ruthie smiled. She'd been happy once when she was a child and her parents alive. It seemed a lifetime ago, or a dream.

The door opened and Mercy came in carrying a tray. 'I've some food if you can manage it?'

'Yes, thank you.' She wasn't ravenous, but Doctor Ashton had implored her to eat when she could.

Mercy placed the tray on a table before helping Ruthie into a sitting position with lots of pillows for support. 'It's roast chicken, potatoes, carrots, cabbage and gravy, and if you can fit it in, there's a jam sponge and custard for afterwards.'

'I'll try my best.' Ruthie liked Mercy Felling a great deal. The woman's kindness helped her to feel less lonely, less afraid.

'Doctor Ashton said, if you're feeling up to it, you can have a nice bath tomorrow. I'll help you.'

'A bath?' Ruthie stared at her as she placed the tray over her lap. She couldn't remember the last time she had a bath. A quick wash from a bowl was the best she'd had for some time.

'We have some fresh clothes for you, too.' Mercy took the covers off the food and the delicious smell wafted over Ruthie.

'Clothes, too?' She couldn't take it in.

'Well, a nightgown to start with, as you're not to be walking about much just yet. We feel that a patient becomes better quicker, when they've had a lovely warm bath and are dressed in a fresh nightgown. In a few days, we'll have you sitting in a chair by the window.'

'I'd like that.'

'Once you're completely well, you'll be moved into one of the dormitories in the main building.'

'How long am I allowed to stay?' she asked nervously, her stomach in knots.

Mercy squeezed her hand. 'Until you are fully recovered, and you have a decent place to go to. We will help you to find a position somewhere and housing.' She stepped back. 'I'll leave you in peace to enjoy your food.'

'I used to work in service for the Coledales' on Bootham.' Ruthie forked up some chicken. 'I liked being in service. Gerald made me give it up.'

'Service?' Mercy nodded, her brow furrowed. 'Interesting. Do you wish to stay in York or move away?'

The idea to move away had played on her mind in the past. To get away from Gerald had always been something she thought about. The bad memories of Micky and getting rid of the baby added to that even more. 'My father grew up in Scarborough. I'd like to find a position there if I could?'

'Scarborough?' Mercy smiled. 'I do love taking the children to the seaside. Leave it with me. Mrs Ashton and I might be able to find you something on the coast. A position in service in a nice house or even a hotel?'

Excitement coursed through Ruthie. 'Really?'

'We can try. Now eat your meal. I'll be back soon.'

While Ruthie ate the delicious food, eating more than she thought she would ever manage, she imagined living by the beach. She'd only been to Scarborough once, when she'd been a little girl and her father took her with him to visit his sick mother. They'd never gone back, but she remembered the sand in her shoes as she ran along the water's edge. The ruins of the castle were high on the cliff above, where the seagulls swooped and dove. The sea that day had been gentle, rolling in, lapping at her feet. She'd squealed just like the children outside were doing. It'd been a day to live on in her memory. Could she dare to dream that one day she might live there? That she could walk the streets her father had done as a youth?

When the door opened, she expected Mercy, but Doctor Ashton came in with that kind smile of his. 'I'm very pleased to see you eating, Miss Benson.'

'It's delicious.'

'We are fortunate to have Mrs Shelton, our cook, working for us.' He sat on the chair beside the bed. 'How are you feeling?'

'Full.' She grinned. He was so handsome she felt a little flushed just looking at him.

'Excellent. Food and sleep will help you heal.' He felt her forehead for her temperature. 'The fever seems to have gone. Your colour and breathing have returned to normal.'

'Mercy said I'm to have a bath tomorrow?' She knew she was dirty. She had dried blood on her from the result of Mrs Cleary's efforts. Her skin and scalp itched.

'Only if you feel up to it?'

'I think I am or will be by tomorrow.'

'A warm bath to relax in is another way of resting. A gentle wash has restoring effects on the mind and body. To feel clean is refreshing and lift's one's spirits.'

'I'd like to wash my hair?'

He nodded. 'You may, however it needs to be thoroughly dried. The last thing we want is for you to catch a chill.'

'I won't. I'm stronger than I look.'

Doctor Ashton's smile was full of sympathy. 'Miss Benson, as you know Mrs Cleary's… work was highly mismanaged. You will be sore and tender in that area for some time. The healing process will take patience. Outwardly, your bruises, and swollen eye will mend, and you will begin to feel more your old self. However, internally, the repair will likely be many weeks. If my wife hadn't brought you here, you would have died from the bleeding, and your brother's assault only exacerbated the matter.'

She nodded, not really knowing the meaning of exacerbated, but understood his implication, and was sobered by the thought of how close to death she'd been. 'I can't thank you and Mrs Ashton enough, Doctor.'

He patted her arm. 'All we need to do is look forward to the future. We start by taking one day at a time. I believe that your brother will serve time in jail for his assault, but you will likely be called as a witness as will my wife. He could have hurt her a lot worse, you know?'

'Yes.' She shivered at the thought of Gerald beating the lovely Mrs Ashton.

'Can you stand up in court as a witness?'

'I don't know.' To be in a courtroom before a judge and maybe be responsible for sending Gerald to prison frightened her. He'd kill her if he ever got out. She knew that without a doubt and her courage failed her. 'I would rather just move away, Doctor.'

'That is understandable. I gather then, that you will not give evidence against Mrs Cleary either? I know it would be difficult for you, but that woman needs to be stopped from hurting others. Mrs Cleary could have killed you and she may have damaged you enough that you may never have children, but I hope not.'

She shook her head, shame coursing through her. 'I can't, sir. To stand up before a judge and admit to being unmarried with a child and getting rid of it? No. I can't do it. They'd think me a whore. I'm not though!' Fear and disgrace made her shake. At this moment she didn't care about possible children in years to come. She doubted she'd ever love again or trust a man enough to come near her so children didn't matter to her right now. But to stand in front of a judge and other men in court and admit her shame, and for it to be reported in the newspapers? No. She'd not do that. 'I'm sorry, Doctor, but I can't do it.'

'Calm down. Do not get upset. No one will make you go, I promise.'

'I thought Micky was going to marry me.' A sob broke from her. 'I'd never have done it otherwise, no matter how many times he wanted to. He said he loved me.' She cried, her heart shattered. 'I loved him. I believed him when he said I was his girl.'

'Hush now.' Doctor Ashton held her to him. 'Men can be cruel and thoughtless and selfish.' He eased her away from him and gave her his white handkerchief. 'But remember, not all men are like Micky or your brother, I promise you.'

She didn't believe him, not really, not the men from her class, but she wiped her eyes and blew her nose.

'You will get past all this, Miss Benson. In time, you will learn to find pleasure in life again.'

Ruthie gazed at the initials embroidered on the handkerchief. 'I just want to start again, Doctor Ashton. Somewhere no one knows me. Somewhere nice. I mentioned to Mercy that I'd like to work in service in Scarborough.'

'Scarborough?' His kind smile returned. 'That's sounds rather lovely. I'm certain Mercy and my wife will do all they can to achieve that.' He grinned. 'They are extremely clever in getting things done that most people wouldn't dare to try.' He stood, waving away the handkerchief when she offered it back to him. 'Keep it. I have no doubt my daughters have embroidered another half a dozen and put them under the Christmas tree for me.'

Mercy breezed in with a bundle of fresh clothes. 'Oh, Joseph. How is our patient?'

Joseph headed for the door. 'She is doing very well.'

'Tomorrow she might be able to join the others for an hour or so to celebrate the day?'

'I should think so if it is only for an hour and she rests straight after.' With a nod he left them.

'I would scare the children.' Ruthie put a hand up to her bruised face.

'They won't batter an eyelid. Sadly, they are used to seeing their mothers with black eyes and bruising.' Mercy laid the clothes on the table by the window and then took the tray from Ruthie's lap. 'I've spoken to Mrs Ashton, and she knows of a lady, a friend of her aunt's, who lives in Bridlington, and may be in need of a parlour maid. What do you think? Shall I write to her?'

Surprised, Ruthie gasped. 'Gracious, that was quick.'

'I'm not saying she has a position, but it wouldn't hurt to write and find out.' Mercy tidied the blankets.

'Bridlington?'

'I know you were thinking of Scarborough, but Bridlington is by the seaside about thirty-five miles from here. Doctor and Mrs Ashton have taken the children there before and said it was a lovely town with a pretty beach. It could be a start for you.'

Ruthie laid back against the pillows, suddenly exhausted. It'd been such an emotional few hours.

'Anyway, I'll leave you to think it over. There's no rush.' Mercy collected the tray and walked to the door.

'Wait.' Ruthie suddenly needed something to look forward to, a dream to cling to and what did it matter where she went as long as she was away from Gerald? 'I think I would like you to write to this lady, please?'

Mercy smiled. 'I'll come back later and we'll both write to this lady, shall we?'

Nodding, Ruthie relaxed against the pillows. Her stomach dipped and swooped with excitement and hope. If she got this job, she'd work hard and make a new life for herself and even feel the sand between her toes again.

The delicious smell of roasting pork filled the air. Victoria stepped beside the spit, where Mrs Shelton basted the sizzling suckling pig with fat. Mr Nevis turned the handle of the spit while Robbie added more wood to the fire beneath it. They'd decided to have the spit outside, near the back entrance to the kitchen. Robbie and the children had cleared the snow from the stone flags and, although it was cold, the sun shone brightly.

'It smells wonderful, Mrs Shelton,' Victoria commended.

'It'll fill some holes in stomachs I should imagine, Mrs Ashton,' the cook replied, dripping the brush in a pot of fat and smearing it over the pig. 'We've got potatoes in the oven as well as turnips. The fruit pudding is waiting for the custard. We're all set.'

'You've done a superb job, Mrs Shelton, and you, Mr Nevis, and Robbie.'

Mr Nevis nodded. 'It's Christmas, Mrs Ashton, the time for us all to enjoy together.'

A group of children ran out of the back entrance of the main building and ran over to them. They gaped in awe at the roasting pig. They were an odd assortment of ages and sex, but they all wore excited expressions.

'Are you all ready for some presents and games?' Victoria asked them.

'Now, Mrs Ashton?' asked a boy that Victoria remembered was called Alan. His mother had arrived a few weeks ago with him and his little brother.

'Yes, why not?' Victoria grinned. 'Go in and tell the others to assemble in the sitting room, quietly though! Remember babies might be sleeping.'

Despite her words, they whooped and yelled and ran back inside.

Victoria shook her head wryly at the adults around the spit.

'You'll not get them to calm down at all today,' Mrs Shelton said.

'No, not likely, but that's allowed for today.' Victoria chuckled.

Walking inside, Victoria held out her hand to Kathleen as she joined her in the corridor. 'Shall we start the present giving? Where's your papa?'

'He's already in the sitting room with the others. I was sent to find you.' Kathleen held Victoria's hand as they walked into the sitting room, which was crowded with women and children, noisy and hot from the fire and so many people in one area.

A large pile of presents sat on a table waiting to be given out. The job always fell to Joseph, and he was waiting for Victoria's nod to begin. Over the previous weeks, Mercy and Victoria had bought small presents for every child and mother staying at the Home.

Victoria stood next to Mercy and Harriet, while their own children helped Joseph hand out the gifts.

'Every year I say we should stop this buying of presents because of the expense,' Harriet murmured. 'Yet, every year I see their faces light up at receiving a gift and I can't go through with it.'

'I know what you mean,' Mercy agreed. 'Look at how happy they are.'

Victoria watched a boy, aged about five, open his gift of a wooden cup and ball. 'For some children this is the first present they have ever had.'

Soon the room was full of excited children as boys played with spinning tops, marbles and tin soldiers, while girls snuggled knitted dolls and little teddy bears. Mothers showed off their gifts, too with each woman receiving a handkerchief, a yard of ribbon and a knitted scarf.

'I think we should have some games soon, while the sun is shining,' Harriet said, looking alarmed at the boisterousness of the children. 'Preferably something outside.'

'Matthew and Seth have hidden apples in the garden,' Mercy said. 'I asked them to do that this morning.'

'Lord, the apples will be as hard as rocks sitting in snow.' Harriet laughed.

'We'd best get them hunting for them, hadn't we?' Mercy grinned.

Victoria stepped up onto a small stool. 'Can I have everyone's attention, please?' She waited for the noise to quieten and a room of expectant faces turned to her. 'Now, we are going to have an apple hunt. Outside in the gardens are lovely apples for the children to find.' She held up a finger as the children chatted excitedly. 'You can only find one apple each. The bigger children are to help the younger ones. All the children are to get their coats on and wait for me by the front door. No one is to go outside until I say.'

As the room emptied of squealing, eager children, mothers followed them out to help put on coats and hats.

Victoria went to Joseph where he sat next to a young woman with a tiny baby on her lap. 'It's your turn after I've finished the apple hunt,' she told him with a laugh.

'I just handed out the presents,' he protested good humouredly.

They both turned to Mercy, grinning.

Mercy stared back at them and then rolled her eyes. 'Very well, I'll organise the next game. Kathleen, Ettie, and my girls you can all help me.'

The room grew much quieter as only the new mothers were left seated. Joseph offered to hold a baby for its mother so she could drink a cup of tea and have a piece of Christmas cake. Harriet sat chatting to another group of mothers with young babies.

Victoria headed to the front hall and weaved her way through the crowd of excited children. At the front door she turned and held up her hand for silence. ‘Now, children, there are rules to this game, and I *will* be watching. Firstly, only one apple per child.’ She eyed some of the older boys, knowing they’d be the ones to cheat. ‘Secondly, you are to stick to the paths that Robbie has cleared. The apples are not in the garden beds, so do not trample my plants which are under the snow!’ She tilted her head, her eyes scanning the eager faces. ‘Older children to help the little ones. Be kind and gentle or your apple will be taken from you!’

She turned and opened the double doors. The brisk clean air hit her as she stepped out onto the top of the steps leading down to the garden. Standing to one side, she smiled to the children. ‘One, two, three, go!’

A dozen or more children ran down the stairs, not caring of the cold and snow and scattered along the paths. The bigger boys ran and fell, laughing, while the girls held hands and skipped along the paths, squealing when some of the boys threw snowballs at them.

Mothers drifted down the stairs, calling out encouragement to the children who spread out amongst the vast gardens. Soon the white virgin snow was trampled, and the gardens were filled with darting children, shrieking happily as they found the hidden apples amongst the trees and garden beds.

An arm sneaked around Victoria’s waist, and she looked up at Joseph. ‘Isn’t that a wonderful sight?’

‘A horde of children destroying the gardens?’ he joked.

She elbowed him softly. ‘No, the happiness.’

He kissed her cheek. ‘It is, my darling, and all thanks to your vision ten years ago.’

'Our vision,' she reminded him, linking her arm through his.

'Come on, let's build a snowman with the children,' Joseph suggested, leading her down the steps.

She paused at the bottom as a carriage turned in through the gates and drove along the drive.

Mr Shaw alighted, his arms full of packages. He bowed to Victoria. 'Mrs Ashton, I have come to call on my daughter.' He indicated the parcels with a nod. 'I have presents for Georgiana and the children.'

'I am certain they will be warmly received, Mr Shaw. Georgiana is inside with the baby, but Iris is out there hunting for apples. I'll send her inside when she's finished.'

'Thank you.' He searched for his granddaughter amongst the crowd of children, then made to walked past Victoria, but hesitated. 'Thank you, Mrs Ashton, for saving my daughter and grandchildren. I am in your debt.'

'You are not in my debt, Mr Shaw. I didn't save her for you,' she said gently. 'My role is to give women without hope a new chance at life. When they have nothing, we offer aid and show them that they are not alone. That is what I and this Home stands for.'

'Indeed.' He seemed a little embarrassed. 'Your work is admirable. I will endeavour to give you whatever support you need in the future to continue your good work.'

'Thank you, Mr Shaw.' She bowed her head in acknowledgement. 'Now, please go inside and spend some time with your daughter. She needs her father.'

Taking a deep breath, Victoria felt relief that Georgiana and her children would have a better future, not all the women she took in had the same outcome.

Chapter Twelve

Victoria woke early on Christmas morning and slipping from the warm bed, and Joseph's arms, she donned her dressing gown and tip-toed downstairs. Opening the curtains, she watched the snow fall gently, covering the footprints made yesterday and giving the trees and gardens another coat of white.

She'd given the maid the day off, and so she quietly went about raking the slumbering embers into a small blaze and adding bits of wood.

Seeing to her own fire would be something her aunt or cousin Stella would never do, nor would she have if her life had been different. But being thrown out of home, she'd learned to adapt and survive in the slums, the lessons learned in those couple of years stayed with her. She was capable of doing so much for herself, despite her marriage to Joseph and resuming the role of a lady from a genteel class, underneath she often felt she was still the young woman who carried water buckets, emptied slops, slept in a bug-ridden bed and who could start a fire.

She turned to study the Christmas tree, resplendent in decorations done by the children. Underneath pretty wrapped presents waited to be torn open by her darling children, but for now they slept soundly upstairs, tired after the busy and exciting day yesterday when they'd joined the other children in playing in the snow and then singing carols after a tasty meal of roast pig.

Her heart flipped at the thought of her educated and well-brought up children mixing with children from the very poorest areas of York, those who'd never had shop-bought toys, or even shoes and socks. However, Kathleen, Ettie and Matthew knew no other way of living. This cottage was their home, but the main building and all their guests was just an extension of their home, just as Mercy's cottage was. She was so proud of the way they helped about the grounds, pitched in with any chores that needed doing, never believing they were better than the other children who arrived in rags with sores, lice and tattered clothes.

If she was a proud mother, she didn't apologise for it. She and Joseph had raised three beautiful children in surroundings not normal for most families. Her children had to share their parents with fifty other women and all their children, and they did it with understanding and kindness.

'What are you doing up so early?' Joseph whispered, tying his dressing gown, his hair messy, stubble darkening his jaw.

'I wanted to get the fire going, so the room was warm for when the children come down.'

'That won't be for hours yet, they were so tired last night.' He wrapped his arms about her. 'Let us go back to bed.'

She grinned at him. 'Matthew will be awake soon, you know he will. He believes there are a set of tin soldiers and new paints under the tree for him.'

'I used to play for hours with my soldiers once I'd painted them,' Joseph reminisced.

'Shall we make some tea before they come down and sit before the fire, just the two of us?' she suggested.

'Sounds perfect. We'll make toast on the fire, too.'

In a short amount of time, they were sitting on cushions before the fire. Joseph held bread speared on long forks near the flames while Victoria poured tea and set out plates with bowls of butter and plum jam.

‘I didn’t expect to be doing this on Christmas morning,’ Joseph chuckled.

‘I did promise you some time together, just the two of us,’ she joked.

He gave her a flippant tut. ‘This wasn’t my meaning.’

‘We are alone, aren’t we?’

‘It’s six o’clock in the morning. I thought I could sleep in a little for once. There are no pregnant mothers due to deliver, no emergencies needing my immediate attention. For the first time in years, I am able to spend Christmas morning with my family.’

‘You can sleep in tomorrow.’ She leaned over and kissed him. ‘For an hour or so. I’ve promised all the children, ours, Mercy’s and the women’s children, we’d take them skating on the duck pond.’

He groaned mockingly. ‘Do I have to go?’

She sipped her tea. ‘You do. It’s a family occasion. You know the girls love it when you hold their hands when they are skating.’

‘Fine.’ He gave in willingly and rotated the bread on the forks. ‘Shall we open a present each?’

Eyebrows raised, she stared at him. ‘That is rather naughty.’

‘The children won’t know.’ He passed the forks to her to hold while he scooted under the tree and pulled out a small box. ‘Merry Christmas, my darling.’

She handed him the forks to take the bread off and while he buttered the slices, she unwrapped the ribbon. Opening the box, her breath caught as she stared at a beautiful sapphire ring. ‘Oh, Joseph.’

‘Do you like it?’

‘It’s glorious.’

‘Try it on.’

She slipped the ring onto a finger on her right hand and gazed at it in admiration. She couldn’t guess how much it must have cost. 'It's too much.'

Frowning, Joseph put down the knife and took her hands in his. 'No, it is not. Darling, you give everything to others. All your time, your energy, your compassion and your support. You raise our children while aiding battered and damaged women and you run a charity that is a beacon of hope to so many others. When do you take time to just be still? To read a book just for pleasure and not to the children? To take a walk by yourself just to smell the flowers? When do you ever stay in bed past six o'clock just because you want to? You give everything you have to everyone else. Allow me to give you something back, a token of how much you mean to me.'

'Joseph…'

'No, my love. Let me spoil you, please? You have only one piece of expensive jewellery that you wear, a piece I bought you nine years ago when Kathleen was born. You refuse to spend money on yourself, so allow your husband to do so. I want to show you how much I love you. We spend such little time together, at least when you wear this ring, you can see it and think of me and know you are adored.'

'I don't need a ring to know how much you love me.' She cupped his cheek in her hand, loving him so much it hurt.

'True, but it pleases me to buy beautiful things for my wife who I treasure above everything.' He kissed her gently. 'You hardly ever allow me to buy you something pretty. This time I just did it. After nearly ten years I think it is due, yes?'

Victoria rested her forehead against his. 'Thank you, my love.'

'I know you'll only wear it on special occasions, like you do with your other piece, and I know I cannot always accompany you when you have fundraising dinners and so on, but at least when you are away from me, you are taking something with you that I gave you.'

'I always have something you gave me when I leave.' She held up her hand with her wedding band. 'This is the greatest gift I'll ever receive.'

He took her hand and kissed the wedding band. 'I was not there when Gerald Benson attacked you. Like the many times before when you've been assaulted, I wasn't there. I'm wounded every time you suffer such abuse. It's becoming harder and harder to see you return home shaken and hurt.'

'It's what we do.' It was her turn to kiss his hands. 'This is how it's always been.'

'And I believe it's time for a change.'

Her stomach lurched. 'What are you saying?'

'From now on, I accompany you when you visit the poor areas.'

'But that isn't practical. You run a hospital. There will be times when you're not free to go with me.'

'Then you do not go until I am.' His tone was deadly earnest, broking no argument. 'I do not ask you for much, Victoria, but I ask you for this. We go together from now on. I can no longer stay behind and wait for you to return not knowing if you are harmed or not.'

Tears burned hot behind her eyes at his distraught face. She nodded, knowing he wasn't asking for much. She could work around his schedule and not only that, but she also wanted him by her side. 'Yes. We'll go together from now on.'

He pulled her in close and they kissed deeply, reaffirming the love they had for each other and giving the silent promise of never taking the other for granted.

Above their heads, they heard the sound of running feet. Matthew's yell to his sisters that it was Christmas made them pull apart and smile at each other.

'Merry Christmas, my love.' Joseph kissed her.

'Merry Christmas, darling.' She turned and laughed as Matthew, Ettie and Kathleen raced into the room.

Acknowledgments

Hello Readers,

Thank you so much for reading *The Slum Angel Christmas* novella and I hope you enjoyed visiting Victoria and the characters from *The Slum Angel* again. I thoroughly relished writing this little story and bringing to life new characters who receive Victoria's care, and we got to see how she and Joseph have evolved and grown. They are such great characters and I wanted readers to see how their lives had continued after the end of *The Slum Angel*.

I am truly delighted to receive such wonderful reviews for my books and lovely messages from readers. They make this author extremely happy! So, please feel free to message me anytime via my Facebook author page.

I'd like to thank my friends and family for their ongoing support, especially my husband who is very encouraging of my career.

I appreciate you all.

Best wishes,

AnneMarie Brear

2021

About the author

AnneMarie was born in a small town in N.S.W. Australia, to English parents from Yorkshire, and is the youngest of five children. From an early age she loved reading, working her way through the Enid Blyton stories, before moving onto Catherine Cookson's novels as a teenager.

Living in England during the 1980s and more recently, AnneMarie developed a love of history from visiting grand old English houses and this grew into a fascination with what may have happened behind their walls over their long existence. Her enjoyment of visiting old country estates and castles when travelling and, her interest in genealogy and researching her family tree, has been put to good use, providing backgrounds and names for her historical novels which are mainly set in Yorkshire or Australia between Victorian times and WWII.

A long and winding road to publication led to her first novel being published in 2006. She has now published over twenty-seven historical family saga novels, becoming an Amazon best seller and with her novel, The Slum Angel, winning a gold medal at the USA Reader's Favourite International Awards. Two of her books have been nominated for the Romance Writer's Australia Ruby Award and the In'dtale Magazine Rone award.

AnneMarie now lives in the Southern Highlands of N.S.W.

You can subscribe to her newsletter by visiting her website: www.annemariebrear.com